THE *boyfriend* WHISPERER

LOVE IS BUT A WHISPER AWAY

LINDA BUDZINSKI

Swoon
ROMANCE

THE BOYFRIEND WHISPERER by Linda Budzinski
All rights reserved. Published in the United States of America by Swoon Romance. Swoon Romance and its related logo are registered trademarks of Georgia McBride Media Group, LLC. No part of this book may be used or reproduced in any manner whatsoever without written permission of the publisher, except in the case of brief quotations embodied in critical articles and reviews.

ePub ISBN: 978-1-944816-85-8 Mobi ISBN: 978-1-944816-86-5
Paperback ISBN: 978-1-944816-90-2

Published by Swoon Romance, Raleigh, NC 27609
Cover design by Danielle Doolittle

To my best friend, Joe. Thank you for making the first move.

THE boyfriend WHISPERER

Chapter
ONE

I sharpen the focus on my binoculars. Are those green peppers or jalapeños?

As Brendon McDonough takes another bite of his pizza, a long, gooey slice of cheese oozes down his chin and drips onto the table. He picks it up, pops it into his mouth, and wipes his face with his sleeve. Charming. What does Jolene see in this dude?

I shake my head and make a note on my tablet: *pepperoni, jalapeños, extra cheese.* When it comes to winning a guy's heart, the devil is in the details—especially when those details pertain to food.

A knock on my car window startles me. Crap. What's Chris doing here? I shut down my tablet and slip the binoculars into my coat pocket.

"Lexi? Is that you?"

I roll down the window. "Hey. Whattup?"

"Nothing. What are you doing?"

"What's it look like?" I point toward my tablet. "I'm … uh … ordering pizza."

"From your car?" He nods toward Italiano's, where Brendon and his friends sit by the back window scarfing down their food. "Why don't you walk in and order it?"

Good question. I open the car door and hop out. My breath makes tiny frosty puffs that disappear into the darkness. I shiver but resist the urge to grab Chris's arm for warmth. Ugh. A year ago I'd have done that without a second thought. He's my best friend, after all, and has been since the third grade. I wheel around on the rubber soles of my Chucks and head toward the door. "Maybe I will. Just trying to save some time, I guess."

Chris follows me. "That makes sense. Who wouldn't want to sit out here in the freezing cold rather than walk into the nice, warm, pizza-scented restaurant where you can tell a real live person what you want and sit down with your soda while you wait for it?"

I turn, stopping so abruptly that Chris runs into me. I ignore the flutter in my stomach. "Why do you do that?"

"What?"

"Make fun of me."

"Make fun? Lexi, I'm playing. You know that. What's up with you lately?"

I want to shove him and tell him to shut up and get out of my headspace, but instead, I sigh. "Nothing's up. Nothing at all."

Chris leans down toward me. I'm five-nine in flats, so

not many guys tower over me like Chris. His light blue eyes shine beneath the parking lot lights, and his blond hair is spiked to hide the cowlick he's fought since we were little. He lowers his voice. "Is it that time of—"

"Omigod!" I stick my finger in his face. "Don't ever ask me that. Got it? Never. I can't believe you almost asked me that." I spin back around and head into Italiano's without waiting for him.

"One slice, please," I tell the girl behind the counter. "Plain cheese." I had a huge dinner and am not the least bit hungry.

"Thought you said you ordered online." Chris tugs at my ponytail as he comes up behind me.

"Tried to. Before I was so rudely interrupted."

He laughs. "Come on. Isn't this better than sitting in your car?"

We fill up our sodas, and I grab a booth as far away from Brendon's table as possible. Discretion is paramount in my line of work.

Chris loosens the paper on his straw and blows it at me. "So where were you this afternoon?"

"Busy." I grab the fluttering paper out of the air and play with it, mainly so I don't have to look him in the eye. "Why?"

"We were trying to get together a game of two-on-two down at the courts. I texted you twice."

"Oh, right. Sorry." I twist the paper around and around on my pinkie finger. "I turned off my phone. I was at the library doing my psych report." That's only a partial lie. The part about the library is true, but I was there to keep tabs on the math team captain for one of my clients. "Sorry I missed it. Who else played?"

Chris grins. "Massey and Briggs. We ended up playing HORSE. I smoked them, obviously."

I laugh. Massey and Briggs suck at HORSE. If it weren't for layups, neither of them would ever score a basket. Even I'd have crushed them, and I'm not as good as Chris. "Now I'm really sorry I missed it."

Chris looks up and gives a low whistle. I follow his gaze to find Alicea Springer and Ty Walker ordering at the counter. Ty has his arm around her.

Chris leans toward me. "Think that's a Boyfriend Whisperer couple?"

I shrug. "Who knows?" Part of me wishes I could fess up and tell Chris everything, but I can't let pride get the best of me. Ty was my toughest assignment ever, and the fact that he's still with Alicea after two months is my biggest success to date. He's super hot, a star forward on the soccer team, drives a BMW, and on top of all that, he's smart. Alicea, meanwhile, was basically a nobody. She's pretty enough, but she's quiet and shy and, until recently, had the self-confidence of an earthworm. At least, I assume earthworms lack self-confidence seeing as how they eat dirt and all.

"It's gotta be." Chris shakes his head. "That chick had more face time with her computer than with guys before they started going out. Ty would never have given her the time of day without some sort of—"

"What do you know?" I kick him under the table. He's right, of course. In fact, he's echoing my exact thoughts when Alicea hired me, but still, his attitude bugs me. "Maybe some guys are better than others at seeing past a girl's image. We're not always what we seem, you know."

"Since when are you an expert on girls?" Chris gives me a teasing grin. "It's almost like you think you are one."

That does it. I slide out of the booth without a word and walk up to the counter to wait for my pizza, leaving Chris to wonder what he's done to tick me off. At least, I hope he wonders. I hope he feels bad for hurting my feelings. I hope he regrets being kind of a jerk tonight. Most of all, I hope he didn't notice the tears that sprang to my eyes as I left our booth.

No. Even more than that, I hope he'll wake up and realize that I am, in fact, a girl.

Chapter
TWO

I dribble down the court and pull to a stop at the three-point line. With one smooth motion, I toss the ball, feeling its rough, rubbery surface roll off my fingers as it launches into a perfect arc. *Whoosh.* Nothing but net. I smile.

It's six o'clock on Thursday morning, and the only people at school right now besides me are the swim team. I decided to come in early and take some reps since I couldn't sleep. I grab the ball and line up on the foul line to practice some free throws. Let's see if I can hit ten out of ten this morning.

My dad used to be a Wizard. Not a Gandalf-Dumbledore kind of wizard, though that would have been cool. He was a backup forward on the Washington Wizards, until about halfway through his second season, at the age of twenty-four, he tore a ligament in his knee. That ended his NBA career, and over the next three years, he got his real estate license, married my mom, and had me. Apparently, Mom had a tough pregnancy and an even tougher labor, so that was the end of the baby-making.

I sometimes wonder if they'd gone on to have a son whether Dad would have bothered to teach me how to play. Maybe he would have focused on my brother and left me to more girly pursuits. That usually makes me glad I'm an only child.

My phone buzzes as I make seven out of seven, and I jog over to the bleachers to pick it up. It's Abigail, my assistant.

Abi: We need to talk.

I shake my head. Abi's great at her job. In fact, there would be no Boyfriend Whisperer Enterprises if it weren't for her, but she can be a pain in my butt. I hit reply.

Lexi: Third-period lunch. F Hall janitor's closet.

Chris was right last night about one thing. I'm no expert on girls. All my friends are guys and have been since I was little. Which—at least compared to most of my classmates—makes me an expert on guys. Which is how I became the Boyfriend Whisperer.

I head back to the free throw line, but Abi's text has shaken me out of my zone, and I miss shot number eight.

I grab the rebound off the backboard and tear down to the other end of the court, zagging and twirling past my imaginary opponents on the way to a perfect layup … except the ball jams between the rim and the backboard. Stuck in limbo. Zero points. Just like my love life.

Abi is waiting for me when I slip into the closet. She's standing next to a collection of mops and brooms, and I swear she's so skinny she blends right in. She starts complaining without so much as a hello. "I can't do this anymore, Lexi. It's too much. I have no social life to speak of, I was late for cheer practice twice last week, and I totally failed my French mid-term."

I give her what I hope is a sympathetic smile. "Abi, Abi, Abi. I told you we'd crazy for a while. We just need to get through Valentine's and then—"

"And then what? And then we're coming up on prom season and then summer of love and then back-to-school and homecoming and the holidays and before you know it we're back to freaking Valentine's!" She says all this in one breath, her eyes widening with every word until she looks like an anime version of a Barbie doll.

I drape my arm around her shoulders. "Breathe. It'll be okay, I promise. Think of all the money we're bringing in.

You'll be able to buy half of Sephora at this rate."

Abi is about as different from me as a girl can get. While my makeup repertoire consists of a single stick of clear lip-gloss, her supply could fill the F Hall janitor's closet to overflowing.

"I know." Impossibly, her eyes widen even more. "Did you know O.P.I. came out with a super-sparkly iris nail polish last month? It'll go great with my—" She shakes her head. "Wait. That's not the point. I mean, it is the point. The money's awesome. But … something has to give. Before I crack."

Crack? As in, talk? Everyone knows Abi works for the Boyfriend Whisperer. They just don't know it's me. "Abi, you promised. You cannot tell anyone."

She shakes her head. "I don't mean like that. I mean I'm about to lose my mind. I should warn you, though. Certain girls are getting curious. Beyond curious. Like, invasive."

"Invasive how?"

"Yesterday I was messaging Libby, trying to find something to do this weekend, when all of a sudden I got this eerie feeling someone was watching me. I turned to find Michelle leaning over my shoulder reading every word. As if I really needed her to know I'm dateless. I'm sure she went and blabbed to half the cheer squad about what a loser I am."

Abi's voice breaks, and I can't help but feel bad. She does deal with a lot of crap. I squeeze her shoulder. "First of all, *you* broke up with *him*. Which makes you a strong girl who knows what she wants and deserves in life, not a loser. Second of all … never, ever message or text me in public, okay? And delete all traces immediately."

She nods. "I know, I know."

"Abi." I grab her arms and stare straight into her eyes. "I need you. You are the public face of Boyfriend Whisperer Enterprises. Those girls are just jealous because you know something they don't."

She manages a small smile. "True. And trust me, I'll never tell."

I breathe a sigh of relief. I need her silence.

Chapter
THREE

Coach Reilly blows her whistle and strolls to center court. "Circle up, girls! Our tournament slot was posted this afternoon. Let's review the schedule."

My stomach rolls around like a ball circling the rim, waiting to drop. The boys' team got their schedule last night. Will we play down in Virginia Beach with them? Maybe if Chris and I can get away from our normal routine, he'll see me differently. Maybe if we could hang out in a fancy hotel lobby, sipping hot chocolate by a roaring fire while the sound of ocean waves crash outside the door, he'll gaze deep into my eyes and see past the eight-year-old tomboy who taught him how to skip rocks and shoot a slingshot and peel hard-boiled eggs into one long twirl and—

"Malloy." Coach throws a ball at me, and I snap to attention just in time to catch it. "Focus, Malloy! What's up with you lately?"

I stare down at the red-white-and-blue Grand View Patriot face painted on center court. That's the same thing Chris asked me last night. "Nothing, Coach. I'm listening."

Coach drones on for a solid ten minutes about the importance of the tournament and how even though we're favored to win our game, we should treat the other team as a viable opponent, and how we need to come together and support each other and play our best and blah, blah, blah. Finally, she pulls out her clipboard and flips to the schedule. "We play early Saturday morning, which means we'll travel down Friday after school. We'll be taking the bus down to …" She squints at her sheet while I hold my breath. "Virginia Beach."

Yes! I drop the ball, sending it skittering across the gym floor. My cheeks flush, but I'm not sure if that's because Coach and the entire team are staring at me or because I can already feel the hot chocolate and the fire—and Chris's gaze—warming me.

Coach shakes her head and continues. "The boys play Saturday night, so you have two options. Our bus will return to Grand View immediately after our game. However, if you want to stay and watch the rest of the tournament and cheer on the boys, you can take their bus home Sunday morning. Assuming you have your parents' permission and we can get enough chaperones."

Sweet. I bite my lip as I flash back to the hotel lobby and Chris's eyes. For the rest of practice, I light up the court, making all four of my three-pointers and eleven out of twelve of my free throws. Watch out, Virginia Beach, and watch out, Chris Broder. It's time for the President and CEO of Boyfriend Whisperer Enterprises to open a case file on herself.

Abi Eisenberg was my first case, before I even had cases, before Boyfriend Whisperer Enterprises even existed.

One day at the beginning of the school year, she walked up to me in the lunchroom. "We need to talk." She says that a lot.

I glanced around to make sure her demand was directed at me and not at Chris or Massey or one of the other guys at our table. "Me?"

"Yes, you. It'll only take a minute."

I shrugged. "Okay."

"Not here." She crooked her finger and turned. "Follow me."

I rolled my eyes at Chris as I stood. This was pre-crush, when Chris and I were strictly friends. I mean, we still are, but back then I was fine with it. In fact, I probably would have been weirded out if anyone had suggested we date.

I followed Abi into an empty science lab. "What's up?"

"Roland Briggs."

"What about him?"

"You two are friends, right?"

"We hang out."

"Does he like me?"

I shrugged. How would I know? We didn't exactly compare love lives between games of pool and pick-up basketball. The closest any of my guy friends came to discussing the opposite sex was the occasional comment about some "hot" girl who sat next to them on the bus or said hi in the hallway.

"I need him to like me."

"What?"

"Let me clarify. I need you to get Roland Briggs to like me."

I frowned. "Why? And how am I supposed to do that?"

Abi gave an exasperated sigh, as though I was being incredibly dense. Which perhaps I was. Romance wasn't exactly my forte.

"Because *I* like *him*. And I don't care how; I just need you to do it."

I sat down on a stool at one of the lab tables and considered this. Clearly, Abi was used to getting what she wanted. "What's in it for me?"

She squinted her eyes and tapped her chin. "I can pay you."

"Pay me? What do I look like, some sort of pimp?"

"What? No! I'm not asking you to set us up in a hotel room. I'm asking you to …" She waved her hands in the air. "Play matchmaker. Coach me on how to get Roland to fall in love with me. You know, like that Cyrano guy we learned about in English lit. I'll be your student, and you'll be my … Boyfriend Whisperer."

And so it began.

Turns out romance is my forte. Or at least, I know how to attract a guy's attention. Four months later, I've set up almost two dozen couples—a ninety-five percent success rate—all while managing to keep my identity a secret. Boyfriend Whisperer Enterprises is the talk of the school, and my price per match is $125, cash only.

Some days I look around at all the couples I've brought together and feel like Cupid himself, but deep down, I know the truth. I'm a fake, an imposter, an emperor with no clothes. Because when it comes to whispering my own crush, I'm a total fail. Stuck in the friend zone with no clue how to escape.

Chapter
FOUR

Dear Jolene:
Thank you for entrusting Boyfriend Whisper Enterprises with your matchmaking needs. If you follow my instructions precisely, you are guaranteed to secure a date with Brendon McDonough within three weeks or your money back. Your first set of instructions is as follows:

Step One: At tomorrow's Anti-Bullying Assembly, sit one row ahead of Brendon, and two or three seats away from him.

Step Two: Five minutes after the assembly begins, catch his eye and yawn, roll your eyes, or otherwise express your boredom.

Step Three: Text him the following quiz questions. (Use extreme caution and do not allow faculty to catch you doing this.)
Madden or Mortal Kombat?
Angry Birds or Plants vs. Zombies?
Anthrax or Mastodon?
Fight Club or Unforgiven?
Adidas or Coogi?
Jalapeños or Black Olives?

Step Four: Give him a smile or thumbs-up after each answer (regardless of the answer).

Step Five: Resume your normal activities. Do not initiate contact with Brendon for the next several days. Additional instructions will be sent at that time.

Good luck, and remember, with Boyfriend Whisperer Enterprises, "Love is but a whisper away."

Sincerely,
The Boyfriend Whisperer
www.boyfriendwhispererenterprises.com

I grin as I hit "send" and save the email into its case folder. This is my favorite part of the job. The research portion is tedious and lonely and—like last night— sometimes freaking freezing. But seeing my data gel into a plan makes all those hours spent sleuthing worthwhile. Tomorrow during assembly, Brendon McDonough will marvel at Jolene's cool taste in music and movies and apps and even pizza toppings. And within a few weeks, he'll ask her out. Guaranteed.

Chris sets his tray down across from mine. It's grilled cheese day, and he's bought five of them. Boy can eat. He's six-foot-three and presumably still growing. Lately, I've noticed his forearms are growing nicely, too. His sleeves are pushed up, and I have to force myself not to stare.

"Did you hear the news?"

He asks this just as I bite into my apple, so I can't help but answer with my mouth full. "What news?"

"Supposedly Duke and UNC will be at the tournament next weekend. Along with UVA and Maryland."

"That's awesome." I swallow and flash him a smile. "Bet you're on their short list."

Chris shrugs and stuffs half a sandwich into his mouth. Literally half a sandwich. "I dunno."

"Are you kidding me? A junior averaging fourteen points a game? They'll be watching you."

He pops open a soda and takes a long swig. When he sets it down, I can see the worry in his eyes. He focuses his attention on the second half of his sandwich as though it's a fascinating culinary delicacy. Fromage Grillé du Cafétéria.

"Come on, Chris, you know—"

"Forget it. Sorry I brought it up."

Fine. I take another bite of my apple. Chris is totally college b-ball material, but the Grand View boy's team is so lame, scouts haven't noticed him yet. In fact, unlike most schools, the attention for the past couple of years has been on our girl's team. And well, specifically, on me. I've had scouts calling since I was a freshman, and as soon as I became a junior this year, the scholarship offers began to roll in.

Come to think of it, I don't want to talk about it either.

Fortunately, Massey arrives at that moment. He sets his tray down and swipes Chris across the back of his head. "What happened to you the other night? I thought we were supposed to play Call of Duty?"

"Dude. Watch it." Chris pushes Massey's arm away, which sends him reeling into the table.

"Hey, you two." I grab our sodas so they don't spill. "Knock it off or I'll report you to Principal Cho. Grand View has a zero-tolerance policy toward violence."

Massey laughs. "Someone paid attention in assembly."

I did. Sort of. When I wasn't watching the Jolene and Brendon Show, which seemed to go according to plan.

Massey sits down. "Seriously, man, where were you? We were about to storm Istanbul."

Chris grunts. "I stopped for pizza and ended up hanging with Lexi for a while." He gives me a strange look, and my face grows warm. We did part on a rather awkward note.

"Are you going to finish that?" Chris points to my half-eaten apple.

"You can't be serious." I hand him the apple, take a deep breath, and broach the subject that's been on my mind since yesterday's practice. "Speaking of the tournament, it'll be fun to get away for a weekend. I mean, Virginia Beach—how cool is that?"

Chris smiles. "Pretty cool."

For one brief, delusional moment, I allow myself to believe his smile means he's imagining sipping hot cocoa with me by a fireplace, but the dream is short-lived.

"Do you know we'll be there the same weekend as the Polar Plunge?" he asks.

"Polar Plunge?"

"Yeah. It's where people jump into freezing-cold water to raise money for Special Olympics."

"Meaning they jump into the Atlantic? In Virginia? In February? That's insane."

"I know!" Chris leans in and lowers his voice so only Massey and I can hear. "I'm totally doing it. You guys should, too. It's in the middle of the afternoon, so it's after your game and before ours."

"What?" Massey stares at Chris as though he's lost his mind. "Coach won't let us do that. Before our game? No way."

Chris shrugs. "What Coach doesn't know won't hurt him. I'm in. Already paid my fifty bucks."

"Wait." I hold up my hand. "Are you telling me you're paying money for the privilege of diving into a frigid ocean?"

"Yep. I told you. It's a charity event. It's all for a good cause. Come on, say you'll do it." His big blue eyes plead with me.

I hesitate. I definitely want to spend as much time as possible with Chris while we're in Virginia Beach, but a Polar Plunge does not have quite the same romantic appeal as sipping hot chocolate by a fireplace. On the other hand, if he's already signed up for it, what choice do I have? "Well, I suppose …"

"Not you, too, Lexi." Massey shakes his head. "Your parents will never go for this."

"As Chris said, what they don't know won't hurt them."

"Right. Like they won't know."

"They won't. Because they won't be there."

"What?" Chris and Massey ask me this in unison. Both look as though I've told them my parents have sprouted wings and flown to the moon.

Mom and Dad have a bit of a reputation at my games as helicopters, which is appropriate because not only do they hover, they sometimes get so loud, the fans around them have to duck and cover their ears. I am so looking forward to a game—and a whole weekend—without them.

"They won't be there," I repeat. "Mom's boss is getting married up in New York, so I'm on my own." I glance at Chris to see whether he understands the significance of this. The two of us, practically unsupervised, for a weekend at the beach.

"This trip just keeps getting cooler and cooler," he says.

"I know, right?" I give him what I hope is a flirty smile.

"So I guess this means …"

"Means what?"

"It means you're in? For the Plunge?"

I sigh and roll my eyes. "Sure. I'm in."

Chapter
FIVE

I spend half the weekend trying to decide on the perfect hairstyle and outfit for next week's Polar Plunge. I am becoming ridiculous on so many levels. When my mother peeks in on me Sunday afternoon, I'm sprawled on my bedroom floor amidst a pile of clothes worrying—of all things—about whether my diving shoes make my feet look too big.

"What on earth?" Mom scans my room. "When did the tornado hit?"

"Sorry. I'll clean it up."

"Honestly, Alexis, what is going on with you lately?"

There it is again. I grit my teeth and force a smile. No sense snapping at her. No, in fact, I need to be extra nice. "I'm fine, Mom. I do have something I need to ask you, though."

Mom wades through the piles, pausing at my trophy case to straighten a few errant pieces. She makes her way over to my bed, picks up a sweatshirt and begins folding it. "What is it, sweetheart?"

I grab a pair of sweat socks and twist them around and around on my left hand. "Saturday after our game, some of the girls are going to … I mean, Coach said if we want, we can …"

"Can what? Spit it out, Lexi."

I take a deep breath. "If we want to watch the rest of the tournament and cheer on the boys, we can stay in Virginia Beach an extra night and come back Sunday."

She squints, and I can practically see her chief financial officer's mind calculating the risks and benefits.

"I'll worry about you being down there alone …"

"Well, it's not like I'll be *alone* alone. There'll be—"

"Of course. Your coaches and the chaperones."

"Exactly." I twist the socks tighter and tighter around my fingers. She has to let me stay. She has to. "Come on, Mom. It would be better than me coming back and spending Saturday night by myself here."

Mom nods. "And there will be scouts. Staying for the other games would give you more time to talk to them."

I stop the twisting. "Right. Scouts."

Mom grabs a t-shirt and tucks it under her chin as she folds. "Chris will be there, right?"

"Yes. What does that have to do with anything?"

She shrugs. "Nothing. I know you can take care of yourself. I'll just feel better knowing he's with you."

I nod, keeping my smile in check. "Of course. He'll

keep me out of trouble."

By now, Mom has a whole pile of folded shirts beside her. She looks at my feet and frowns. "What's with the diving shoes?"

"Oh, nothing." I pull them off and toss them into a corner. "I was … checking to see whether my feet have grown since last summer."

A lame explanation, especially since they stretch, but Mom seems satisfied. "I suppose it's fine. Make sure you keep your phone charged so you can text and let us know how you're doing."

"Will do. Thanks, Mom."

She leans forward. "Now for the real question: Are you ready for the game? Have you worked out the problem with your fade shot or does Dad need to drill you on it?"

I shake my head. "I'm getting better at them. And I'm seriously killing it on my free throws. Went eleven for twelve at practice the other day."

Mom's eyebrows shoot up. "Excellent. Eleven stars for you."

We both laugh. When I was little, Mom and Dad awarded me with a glow-in-the-dark star for every basket I made during my games. I stuck them on the ceiling above my bed until I had a whole galaxy of success shining over me. Back then, those stars meant everything. I'd fall asleep counting them night after night.

Mom stands to leave. She pauses at my bedroom door. "Do you need any spending money for the trip?"

I shrug and look away. "Sure. Twenty dollars?"

"You sure that'll be enough?"

"I think so. If not, I still have some babysitting money left over from last month. I'll be fine." She and Dad have no idea that I have my own business and an investment account with more than two thousand dollars in it. I feel bad keeping it from them, but to echo Chris's words, it's for a good cause.

Mom closes the door, and I jump up and do a little happy dance. It's happening. Me, Chris, Virginia Beach. Sweet. As I grab the pile of shirts to put away, my phone buzzes. It's a text from Chris.

```
Chris: My shift ends at 4. Wanna see
the new x-men movie?
```

I grin and my heart flutters in my chest. Why, yes. Yes, I do.

Chapter
SIX

Chris works at the movie theater, which means he gets free tickets and even free popcorn sometimes. To me, it seems like the best job a guy could have, but he insists it's not all glitz and glamour.

"The chunks of hotdog were the worst," he's saying to one of his co-workers as I walk up to him at the snack counter at the end of his shift.

"Hotdogs?" I ask.

"Hey." He grins when he sees me. "Forget it. You don't want to know."

"Oh, but I do."

Chris shakes his head. "No. You don't. Little kid had a … reaction to some of the 3D effects."

"Ew. Got it." My gag reflex kicks in and I hold up my hand to keep him from divulging the details.

"You must be Lexi." His coworker, a skinny guy with

bushy black hair, leans forward on the counter, his eyebrows raised so high they disappear behind the hair. "I've heard a lot about you." He grins at Chris, whose cheeks redden as he scowls and turns away.

I shrug and mumble something about not believing everything you hear. I should be used to it by now, but I'm always still surprised when kids from other schools know who I am. I'm also a little surprised to see it bother Chris— he's usually my biggest cheerleader—but he's been sensitive about basketball lately so maybe he's tired of everyone fussing over me.

We order two large popcorns—because one can never have too much popcorn at the movies—and make our way in. It's one of those theaters with huge reclining chairs that slide all the way out and back, with big trays and cup holders for our stuff. We settle into our seats well before the movie's start time. Chris has seen most of these trailers a dozen times, but he still wants to watch each one. He says it's all part of the movie-going experience.

"That one's on the top of my list," he whispers to me after an intense preview for a Russell Crowe flick. "We have to see that."

"Definitely." I sneak a peek at his profile, strong and beautiful in the glow of the screen. We've seen hundreds of movies together over the years, and his eyes still shine as brightly as when we were kids while he watches. Chris and I love the same kinds of movies. The more action, the better—gunfights, car chases, badass martial arts moves. We have a running joke where we always bet on the number of explosions we'll see before the flick starts.

About halfway through the feature, as I'm losing myself in the X-Men's exploits to save Earth from annihilation, a phone rings. It's the guy next to me, and it's super loud, with a ringtone that blares like a bullhorn. I jump in my seat. For real? Did he not see the four reminders to turn off his phone before the movie? Even worse, he answers it.

"Hello? Hey, man. How's it hanging?" He's not even whispering. It's like he's sitting at home watching Netflix and chatting with his bestie.

I look over at Chris in disbelief, but for some reason, he's staring at his own phone. I take a deep breath and lean over. "Excuse me. Maybe you should take that outside." I say it as sweetly as possible, but the guy gives me the finger and keeps talking. Whoa. I smell beer on his breath and realize he's slurring his words. Before I can figure out how to respond, Chris is standing in front of him.

"Buddy, you need to hang up or leave. And you might want to apologize to my friend for disrespecting her."

I'm not sure who's more shocked—the guy or me. Chris has never been the type to pick a fight. In the seventh grade, a couple of boys made fun of a dorky hat he wore, and I swear he would have let them pick on him for weeks if I hadn't stepped in one day and threatened to kick their butts.

Phone Dude tucks in his recliner and stands. Chris has about four inches on him, but the guy's arms are massive, and a sinister snake tattoo curls out from under his shirt and up the back of his neck.

By now, everyone in the theater has forgotten the movie and is watching the live show playing out in Row H. Chris lifts his hands in the air in surrender mode but stands his ground. "I don't want any trouble. I just want to let all these nice people enjoy their movie."

The guy surveys the room. He wouldn't do anything stupid in front of so many witnesses, would he? On the other hand, maybe now that he has an audience, he'll decide to show off how tough he is.

He steps toward Chris and flexes his right hand, but before he can take a swing, three theater staff appear out of nowhere and surround him. "Show's over, man," says one of Chris's managers. "Let's go."

The guy scowls, but he backs off, grabs his coat, and stalks out. He knocks over some poor lady's soda on his way down the steps, and the manager rushes over to assure her they'll replace it.

The audience breaks out in cheers, and the kid on the other side of Chris gives him a fist bump as he sits down.

"Holy crap," I say as we push back our seats. "I can't believe you took that dude on. He was a beast."

Chris shrugs and shows me his phone—an SOS text to his manager. "I knew Tony and those guys would show up pretty quick. Also, I had no idea how big the guy was until he stood up."

I start to take a sip of my soda, but Chris leans over and grabs my cup to stop me. "Hey." His voice is soft. "Sorry I didn't get the apology out of him."

My mouth goes dry as his hand covers mine, and I have to force myself not to stare at his lips. "You did great. Seriously."

The rest of the movie rolls by in a blur. I've never been the damsel-in-distress type, but that was freaking hot. As far as I'm concerned, the X-Men have nothing on Chris Broder.

Chapter
SEVEN

Dear Jolene:

Nice job at the assembly. You're well on your way to claiming Brendon as your boyfriend. Your next steps are simple:

Step One: Wednesday after school, Brendon will be practicing drums with his metal band. You are to send him the following text:

Boxers or Briefs?

Do not acknowledge his response.

Step Two: On Friday, before the pep rally, Brendon will most likely stop at his locker in C

Hall. Walk by, catch his eye, and smile.

Note: This is not to be a timid smile. It is to be BOLD and BRILLIANT and shout: "I AM A CONFIDENT, BEAUTIFUL GIRL, AND ANY BOY IN THIS SCHOOL WOULD BE LUCKY TO DATE ME."

Step Three: At the pep rally, sit somewhere within his sightline. Make no further contact until you receive my next set of instructions.

Sincerely,
The Boyfriend Whisperer
www.boyfriendwhispererenterprises.com

P.S. You ARE beautiful, and any boy at Grand View WOULD be lucky to date you. Don't forget that!

"And finally, give it up for your defending state championship Grand View Patriots girls' basketball teeeeeam!"

Principal Cho calls my teammates out one by one at the pep rally. He announces my name last, and I dribble across the court, through a tunnel made up of the cheer squad as well as both the boys' and girls' teams, and stop at the top of the key to throw Chris an alley-oop.

He sails toward the basket, his muscles rippling as he reaches out, snatches the ball out of the air, transfers it from one hand to the other, and stuffs it through the rim. Magnificent.

I remember the precise moment I fell in love with Christian Broder. It was this past October when a bunch of us decided to play a pick-up game at the courts down at Claymore Park. It was a warm day, and Chris took off his shirt. I vaguely wondered when he'd developed pecs. I tried to defend against him on a drive to the basket, but it seemed he'd gained six inches on me overnight. He swerved around, up, and past me, and ... wham. His first dunk shot.

It was perhaps the most beautiful move I'd ever seen on a basketball court. Or anywhere. Ever. I could barely breathe. Had to fake a cramp in my leg and take myself out of the game. Now, watching him soar through the air again, I have that same gut reaction. I struggle to pull myself together as he runs up and gives me a high-five.

"Nice toss, Malloy."

"Nice tip in, Broder."

He laughs. "Yeah, right. Tip in. I hear you." He drapes his arm across my shoulder. "I have a great feeling about this weekend."

I nod, unable to form words, and the rest of the pep rally swirls by in a whirlwind of pompoms and victory chants.

Afterward, as I head toward the girls' locker room trying to analyze whether Chris's comment meant he had a good feeling about the tournament, the scouts, the Polar Plunge, or maybe—just maybe—us, Roland Briggs grabs my arm and pulls me to the edge of the hallway. "What was in that envelope?"

"Envelope?" I feign ignorance, but I know exactly what he's talking about. Abi collects all the money from my clients and delivers their payments to me every Friday morning behind the school's recycling station. No idea how Briggs saw us, unless he followed her.

"I saw Abi hand you an envelope this morning. What was in it?"

I shake my head and stall. "Dude, you need to let her go."

"Did it have something to do with me? Or with another guy?"

"What? No. The world does not revolve around you, Briggsy. Nor, for that matter, other guys." I want to say, "*Abi's* world doesn't revolve around you," but decide that would be too cruel. He does love her, in his own immature way.

"Well then, what was it?"

"It was nothing." I pull my arm loose and start walking. "Get a life, would you?"

He follows me. "Wait a minute. Of course." He snaps his fingers. "It had something to do with the Boyfriend Whisperer, didn't it?"

I say nothing, but I must look guilty because Briggs's eyes light up. "No way." A huge grin spreads across his face.

"I don't believe it. You've hired the Boyfriend Whisperer, haven't you?"

I glance away. I'd rather him believe that than figure out the truth.

"Oh, man. Who ever would have thought? Lexi Malloy is in love." Briggs dances around me. "Who's the lucky guy? Anyone I know?"

"Shut up. This isn't about me. This is about you, stalking Abi. It's not attractive, and it's not going to win her back." I pause at the locker room door. "Listen. If you want to get back together with her, you need to treat her like a princess. Take her to dinner, buy her flowers, post sweet pictures of the two of you on Instagram. She loves that stuff."

Briggs raises his eyebrows. "How do you know? Are you and Abi suddenly best friends?"

"Let's just say I observed her enough while you two were together to figure out the type. Take it from me. If you want to catch your own rebound, you need to put yourself in position." As I open the door and step inside, I leave him with one thought: "Lucky for you, Valentine's Day is coming up."

Chapter
EIGHT

I grab a seat at the back of the bus and spread out so no one will sit with me. Not that they'd want to. It's not that my teammates don't like me, or that I don't like them. I do. They're nice people. But I hate girl drama, and our team tends to have more drama than a Shakespearean tragedy. Last I heard, Keisha and Marty were fighting over some guy, and Paige, April, and Shauna were mad at Carmella because she said something to someone about some stupid thing I'm sure nobody even remembers anymore.

When guys get pissed, they curse, call each other idiots, make suggestions about performing certain crude and anatomically impossible acts, and it's over. They move on. Girls can hold grudges for entire seasons. Ain't nobody got time for that, least of all me.

I crank up Mumford & Sons on my iPod and pull up

the Boyfriend Whisperer Enterprises files on my tablet. With Valentine's ten days away, I need to plot out some big moves for my clients.

I start with Jolene. I watched Brendon staring at her this afternoon during the pep rally. He's falling hard. No need to play it subtle. He likes spicy food, so Red Hots are an obvious choice, in a heart-shaped tin. What should the card say? Something super flirty. "Let's heat it up on Valentine's." No … "spice it up." I jot that down and move on to my next client.

Just as I'm picking out a sweet YouTube link I want her to send her BF-to-be, Coach Reilly pulls my earbud out and scares me half to death.

"Malloy! I'm talking to you. What are you working on?"

I slam my tablet shut. "What? Homework. Sorry. What do you need?"

She shoves my backpack to the floor and plops down beside me. "Let's talk about tomorrow. We're expecting scouts from all over. Rumor has it someone from U Conn might even turn up."

She pauses as if to gauge my reaction, so I force a smile. "U Conn? Wow. That's great."

She leans in. "There'll be a lot of buzz in that arena. Parents, coaches, other players. They'll all be talking about the scouts and about you and your future. Here's the thing: You need to ignore them."

"Ignore them."

"Exactly. You have one job tomorrow, and that's to play the best game Alexis Malloy knows how to play. Run, pass, shoot, rebound. That's it. The rest is static. Ignore the static."

"Got it. Static."

Coach furrows her brow. "You nervous?"

"Maybe a little."

She pats my arm as she stands. "A little nervousness is good. You've got this, Malloy. You can do it."

I smile and slump back into my seat. The fact is, I'm not at all nervous. I only said that so she wouldn't launch into a lecture about being too cocky. She's forever vacillating between warning me not to be too nervous and not to be too cocky, when in reality, I'm neither. The truth is, when it comes to college scouts, I just wish they'd leave me alone.

Chapter
NINE

In my dream, I make shot after shot, but the scoreboard never budges. Jump shots, lay-ups, fades—all perfectly executed, yet worth nothing. Zero. Zero. Zero. Zero. My parents and coaches and teammates all scream at me. *Come on, Lexi! What's wrong with you? Score some points! We need points!*

I wake with a start, my chest tight as though a vise is squeezing my heart, my lungs, my ribs. I'm in a strange room, with strange noises. It takes me a moment to realize the room is at the Virginia Beach Sheraton, and the noises are Carmella's snores. I moan, roll over, and pull the blanket over my head. Stupid dream. I've had it many times, over and over again, ever since I was little. But it always seems so real.

By the time Chris and the rest of the Grand View boy's team stroll into the arena, my team is up 46-28 with two minutes left on the clock. Seriously? They want us to stay tonight and cheer for their sorry butts, and they can't even make it by halftime for our game?

I know I should let it slide. No doubt they hit a bunch of traffic in Fredericksburg and had trouble checking into their rooms and yadda, yadda, yadda. But still.

The other team calls a timeout, and we break toward the bench. I sneak a peek across the court at Chris, who smiles and waves and gives me a huge thumbs-up as he points toward the scoreboard. I turn back around and ignore him. Sixteen of those points were mine—one three-pointer, three free throws, and five two-point shots, not that I'm counting—and he missed them all.

I score three more points before the final buzzer. As my teammates celebrate, I pull Coach aside. Somehow I need to get out of watching the afternoon games so I can do that stupid Polar Plunge. "I don't feel well."

"You sure? You tore it up today."

"Thanks, Coach. But, yeah. It's a stomach thing. Probably that garlic-and-onion bagel I ate this morning. Think I'll go back to the hotel and take a nap."

Coach puts her hand to my forehead. "The U Conn scout might want to talk to you. You sure you can't tough it out?"

I feign disappointment as I clutch at my stomach. "It sucks. But I'm sure."

Before Coach can finish nodding, I'm out of there. I head back to my room to change and pack a bag with my swimsuit, wet shoes, and a towel. I brush my teeth three times—because garlic-and-onion bagel—and make my way downstairs for my secret rendezvous with Chris. As I enter the lobby, I gaze longingly at the fireplace. Why couldn't it be *that* kind of secret rendezvous?

"Lexi!" Chris is standing by the door, holding a huge canvas bag and grinning like the Cheshire Cat. "Ready to do this?"

"Where's Massey?"

"He bailed. Coward."

I peer into his bag. Four towels and a wool blanket. Boy's serious. "Nice of you to make it to our game this morning."

"Of course. Wouldn't miss it."

I cross my arms. "You almost did."

Chris groans. "Right. Blame Briggsy for that. Slept through his alarm. We had to wait a half hour for his lazy butt. And of course, we got backed up in Fredericksburg."

"Of course."

"Hey." Chris places his hand on my shoulder, sending a shiver through me. "You're not mad, are you? I wanted to be there. You know I did."

"I know." Part of me wants to push Chris away, and

part of me wants to pull him close and kiss him. And for some reason that I cannot fathom, part of me wants to cry. I blink hard and try to ignore that part of me. "Did you know you've only missed six of my games since I started playing in the fourth grade? And that was usually because you had a game at the same time."

"I did not know that, but it doesn't surprise me that you do." Chris sighs. "What do you want me to say, Lexi? I'm sorry."

"It's okay." And it is. For whatever reason, knowing that he knows that I know he missed most of this morning's game and that I'm keeping track makes me feel better.

Chris motions toward the front the door. "All right, then. Ready to take the plunge?"

I steal one last yearning glance at the fireplace and sigh. "Sure. Let's do this."

Chapter
TEN

The beach is crowded. In February. We're surrounded by people whose idea of a good time is taking an ice bath. Two guys, or maybe girls, wearing polar bear costumes give everyone high fives as they check in. There's a huge medical station and a bunch of dudes who look like Navy SEALs meandering around in their dive suits. I imagine they're supposed to make me feel safer, but safety isn't really my top concern. I'm not so much worried about drowning as I am about FREEZING MY FREAKING BUTT OFF FOR NO APPARENT REASON.

Excuse me. For a good cause.

I head into the women's changing tent and slip on my bathing suit. My legs are as white as the sand. Perhaps a shade lighter. Ugh. I huddle beside a heat fan for a few moments before going out to meet Chris.

The pecs. Oh, my. I haven't seen them in months. And now he has abs, too. As in, sweeter-than-Dew, six-pack abs. Holy cow. He runs up and grabs my hand, and for a moment I'm too stunned to move.

"Come on," he says. "The sooner we get in, the sooner we get out."

First sensible thing the boy has said all week. We take off and splash in up to our thighs. That's when I falter. I can't go any farther. The water is beyond freezing.

"It's not a Plunge until you plunge," Chris shouts. He insists we go big or go home. Heads under.

I rub my arms. "Cold. Cold. Cold."

"Come on, Lexi. You got this." He dives into a wave.

I can't do it. I want to, but I can't. Every inch of my body is rebelling.

Chris surfaces about fifteen feet away and calls to me. "It's not so bad once you're in."

We both laugh. I used to say that to him at the pool all the time. He hated it. He was such a skinny kid, and kind of awkward. Who knew he'd grow up to become this hot, sexy, Polar Plunging dude?

I take a deep breath—or as deep as my shivering body will allow—and dive into the next small wave. Holy cow. Freaking freezing.

That's it. Time to get out. I look around for Chris and see that he's already halfway to shore. Guess he had the same idea.

My legs plod slowly through the swirling water, despite the fact that my brain is shouting at them to hurry up. The air feels much, much colder now that I'm soaked, so

I dip in up to my shoulders for "warmth." All I can think about is that heat fan in the women's changing tent. A wave knocks me back, and I try to regain my footing. As I struggle to propel my weakening legs forward, a group of about six middle-aged women holding hands rush toward me, squealing and laughing and blocking my way.

Suddenly I'm sinking. I can't feel my calves. I try to will them to move, but they seem somehow disconnected from the rest of my body. The instruction sheet they gave us at check-in said not to stay in the water for more than five minutes without a wet suit. It hasn't been that long, has it?

I look around for a diver, but can't see past the gaggle of ladies splashing and screeching.

"Help. I need some help." My teeth are chattering so hard, and my body is shaking so much, I'm not sure whether I'm actually shouting the words or just thinking them. Not that anyone could hear me over these women.

I wave at one of them, and she waves back. "Crazy, aren't we?" She laughs and turns back to her friends.

Wonderful. I try to swim toward shore, but my arms are so cold and stiff, they can't compete with the small breakers swirling around me.

I roll over to float on my back, but my legs are two dead weights pulling me down. I swallow a mouthful of saltwater, and that's when panic sets in. I start to flail. Is it true that people go down three times before they drown? Did that count as my first time? Am I going to die at seventeen? Doing a stupid Polar Plunge? My parents will be so pissed. And I'll never get to franchise the Boyfriend Whisperer. And I'll never know what it's like to kiss Chris. And—

A violent wave startles me. I'm being pulled out to my death at sea. Only it's not a wave. It's Chris, and he's pulling me up onto the beach. The parts of me that aren't completely frozen thrill at the harsh scratch of sand.

Chris wraps a towel around me, and a blanket. And himself. He rubs my cheeks with his hands. "Are you okay? Are you okay? Lexi, say something."

My teeth won't stop chattering, and my lips won't form actual words.

"This was so stupid. What was I thinking? Stupid, stupid, stupid."

I've never seen such fear in Chris's eyes. He continues berating himself while feeling slowly returns to my extremities.

Finally, I speak. "I'm okay."

"You're okay?"

"Yeah."

Relief washes over his face as he tries to help me stand. "Come on. We need to get you to the medical station."

I shake my head. "We can't do that. They'll call our parents." We'd get in so much trouble, especially Chris. His coach would no doubt bench him tonight, and he'd lose his chance to play in front of the scouts. My mouth isn't quite able to articulate all that, so I simply say, "Coach Wallis will kill you."

He shakes his head. "So? I don't care."

He should. This is his best chance of the year to impress the top teams in the region. "Let's just hang here." With your arms wrapped around me. I lean my face into his chest and close my eyes as he rubs my arms and back.

"Lexi, I shouldn't have made you do this. I'm sorry."

I shake my head. "It's okay, seriously. It was fun. Or at least … different. And I'm fine."

He tilts my face toward his. "You scared me half to death; you know that? Are you sure you don't want to get checked out by the EMTs?"

I shake my head. "Not necessary."

"I am so sorry."

"Stop apologizing."

"How can I make it up to you? Tell me. I'll do anything."

I rest my head on his chest. I can't tell him what I really want, so I name the next best thing. "Hot chocolate."

Chapter
ELEVEN

I pluck a marshmallow out of my cup and pop it into my mouth. Mmm. Perhaps the yummiest marshmallow I've ever tasted.

Chris and I came back to the hotel, changed, and found a couch by the fireplace. His game starts in less than two hours, so we have just enough time for a cup of cocoa and, I'm hoping, some serious eye-gazing. Despite the fire, I'm still shivering, so Chris drapes his jacket across my shoulders. So far, so good.

"How come you were so scared back there?" I tuck my chin and peer up at him in what I hope is a flirtatious manner.

"I don't know. Maybe the fact that your lips were blue? Or that you weren't speaking? Or that your legs seemed paralyzed?"

"That was the weirdest part—losing the feeling in my calves." I lean toward him. "You saved my life, you know. I was going down."

"Don't say that."

"It's true."

Chris blanches. I place my hand on his and bat my lashes. "First the guy in the movie theater and now this. You're my hero." My tone teases, but I'm hoping to appeal to the protector, the conqueror, the he-man inside of him.

Chris shakes his head and scowls. "Right. Except the guy in the theater never did apologize, and today never even would have happened if I hadn't pushed you into it. Some hero." He starts to pull his hand away, but then he stops and looks into my eyes. "Lexi?" His stare is intense. Is he gazing?

"Yes?"

"Did you get sand in your eyes? It seems like you're blinking a lot."

I shrink back. "Oh. Maybe." Why do I suck so badly at this? My flirting advice always looks so good on paper, and it seems to work for everyone else, but whenever I try it, I somehow manage to—

"Is anyone sitting here?"

Lindsay LaRouche, one of the cheerleaders, is standing in front of us, pointing at the three inches that separate Chris and me. I frown at Chris, but he shrugs and scoots away.

"Have a seat." He fluffs up a pillow against the seat back.

Seriously?

She squeezes between us and turns to Chris. "Where have you been all afternoon? I've been looking for you."

"You have?" His face reddens. Or at least, I imagine it reddening based on the tone of his voice. I can't actually see it since the back of Lindsay's red-white-and-blue uniform is about four inches from my face.

No, Lindsay. No one was sitting here because it's a small couch, maybe even a loveseat, meant for two people to cuddle up and enjoy the fire. I daydream for a moment about spilling my hot chocolate all over her bright white cheer shoes but decide that would be a waste of perfectly good cocoa.

Lindsay squeals at something Chris says and somehow manages to scoot even closer to him. Another couple of centimeters and she'd be in his lap. "What are you doing tonight after the game?"

My heart sinks. Is she asking him out? Lindsay is everything I'm not. She has perfect hair, a perfect smile, a perfect body. And apparently, she is not at all awkward when it comes to flirting with Chris.

He scoots forward and peers at me. "I think a few of us are planning to check out the Tex-Mex place across the street, right, Lexi?"

"Um, I'm not sure if that's a firm plan or—"

"You can come if you want," he says. "Should be fun."

I hold my breath. *Please say no. Please say no.*

"Sounds great, but I probably shouldn't. A bunch of the cheerleaders are planning a girl's night out." Lindsay leans toward him, and it's obvious from her tone that she wants him to beg her to join us.

Fortunately, Chris is oblivious. "Too bad. Maybe next

time." He glances at his phone. "I should probably take off. Warm ups start in twenty minutes."

Lindsay pouts. "Good luck. I'll be cheering for you."

Well, duh.

Chris stands, and for a brief moment he reverts back to his once-scrawny younger self. His legs shift clumsily beneath him and he stammers. "Thanks. I … I guess I'll see you over there."

He starts to leave, then turns back around and points to me. "I almost forgot."

My heart quickens, and I smile up at him. Forgot what? To tell me how much it will mean to him to have me in the stands cheering as well?

"My jacket."

Oh. Right. I strip it off and hand it to him. As he slips it on over his jersey, Lindsay jumps up and gives him a quick hug. "For good luck!"

"Wow. Thanks." Chris's face burns as red as the stripe in his jacket as he pulls away. "We probably need it."

He takes off without another word to me. The hot chocolate sits heavy in my stomach, and the sticky sweet taste of marshmallow coats my throat.

Chris may not or may not have fallen for Lindsay's flirting tactics. He may or may not even understand she's into him. But one thing is certain: He is fully aware of the fact that Lindsay LaRouche is a girl.

Chapter
TWELVE

The Tex-Mex place is loud in every sense of the word. It's a cacophony of bright yellow and orange walls, tables decorated with murals, patterned tiles on the floor, and rhythmic mariachi music pulsing through the sound system. The entire boys' team and a few of my teammates from the girls' team have taken over the front half of the restaurant, and we are doing our part to add to the ruckus.

"Dude, try a few drops. It's not that hot." I hold out the bottle of Tabasco sauce, but Chris pushes it away.

"I'd need a whole pitcher of Mountain Dew to use that stuff."

I roll my eyes as I shake the sauce onto my taco salad. "Wimp. Wimp, wimp, wimp."

Chris takes a bite of his extra mild chicken burrito. "Guilty as charged," he mumbles, mostly to himself.

"Come on." I tilt the bottle over a slice of his chicken. "One drop. You might like it."

He looks doubtful, but he relents. "One drop."

By now our whole table is watching. Massey leans in and slaps him on the back. "You got this, bro. You can do it."

Chris pushes him away. "Shut up." He nibbles at the chicken and nods. "Not bad."

He tries to play it cool, but I notice his hand reaching for his Dew and can't help but smile. He's adorable, even when he is being a wimp. "Well done." I give him a high five and wave off the onlookers. "Excitement's over, folks. Nothing more to see here."

"I'd say the excitement's just getting started." Jerod Wilkins appears at the front door. Jerod plays center for Pine Bridge, one of our rival schools from back home. He, Chris, and I hung out together last summer at basketball camp.

"Hey, man, how's it going?" Chris stands and gives him a bro hug. "How was your game?"

Jerod pulls up a chair from the next table, swivels it around, and sits down next to me. "Close, but we pulled it out. You?"

Chris shrugs. "We lost. Bad."

"Chris lit it up, though," I pipe in. "Nine baskets and four assists. And a bunch of scouts were there to see it."

Jerod turns toward me. "Speaking of great games, that shot you took at the halftime buzzer was sick."

"You saw that?"

"Wouldn't have missed it."

I raise one eyebrow at Chris and give Jerod my sweetest

smile. "Thank you. I appreciate that. I really do."

"I tried to track you down afterward, but you left." Jerod is staring at me with his big dark eyes. He stared like that sometimes at basketball camp, but I never thought much of it. I just assumed he was an intense guy.

"Sorry I missed you."

"Yeah. It's been a while." He takes a lock of my hair and lets it fall through his fingers. "Your hair's gotten long. I don't think I've ever seen it down before. Looks good on you."

My face grows warm. "Thanks." I glance over to see whether Chris has taken notice of Jerod's obvious flirting, but he's guzzling down his drink.

"So where'd you disappear to?" Jerod asks.

I shift in my chair. "I, um, wasn't feeling well. A stomach thing."

Jerod glances at my taco salad smothered with Tabasco sauce. Ugh. Fortunately, I don't have to explain, because, at that moment, the already impressive decibel level in the restaurant practically doubles. The cheer squad has arrived. Apparently "girl's night out" means, "put on a bunch of makeup and semi-revealing outfits and find the guys."

I expect Lindsay to make a beeline toward Chris, but she barely even acknowledges him as she takes a seat two tables away.

For the rest of the evening, I split my attention between listening to Chris and Jerod break down the tournament scouting action and keeping tabs on the number of times Lindsay checks out our table, which isn't that many. Maybe I was wrong about her liking Chris, or maybe she has a short attention span when it comes to guys. Or maybe she's playing hard to get. How many times have I advised my clients not to initiate contact?

Abi is sitting next to Lindsay, and she seems miserable, probably because two of the other cheerleaders are hanging all over Briggs. For two seemingly simple people, Abi and Briggs have a very complicated relationship. I want to go over there and smack him upside the head. This is exactly the kind of stuff he cannot afford to pull if he wants to get back together with her.

When the waitress finally brings our checks, Jerod throws some cash on the table and stands to leave. He leans down and puts his hand on the back of my chair. "Catch you later, Lexi. Or maybe sooner?" He walks away without waiting for an answer. Thank goodness. I have no idea what to say to that.

I glance over for Chris's reaction, but he's studying his check, frowning as though he's trying to calculate the square root of Pi rather than a simple twenty percent tip. I sigh. It felt nice to have someone flirt with me, but it would have been even nicer to see a hint of jealousy from across the table.

As I count out my share of the bill, Briggs plants himself in Jerod's chair. He's grinning from ear to ear and practically bouncing in his seat. "So was that the dude?" he asks.

"Was who what dude?"

"The dude who just left. Was he the Boyfriend Whisperer dude?"

"What?" Chris finally looks up from his check.

Briggs slaps the table. "You haven't heard? Lexi hired

the Boyfriend Whisperer. That was the dude, wasn't it?"

"Shut up." The Tabasco sauce is burning up my stomach, my throat, my face. "Don't listen to him. He doesn't know what he's talking about."

"It's true. I saw her hand Abi an env—"

"I said, shut it!" I clap my hand over his mouth. "Mind your own business, Briggsy."

"It's cool." Chris folds the check in half. "Jerod seems like a good guy. If you want to go out with him—"

"Omigod. I do not want to go out with him. Briggs doesn't know what he's talking about."

But Chris isn't listening. He's folding his check up smaller and smaller—into quarters, eighths, sixteenths. "I mean, personally, I don't think you need some stupid Boyfriend Whisperer to make it happen, but if that's what you want to do, why shouldn't you? He's—"

"Enough." I grab the check away from him, and Chris finally shuts up. "You really think I should go out with Jerod?"

He shrugs. "If that's what you want."

"Because it did seem like he was flirting with me."

"Oh, he was." Chris imitates Jerod's smooth voice. "Nice halftime shot. Love your hair. Catch you sooner, babe."

So he was paying attention. He heard every word Jerod said to me. The bad news is, none of it made him jealous.

"Well, then. Maybe I'll text him when we get back home."

Chris looks away. "You should. Nothing's stopping you."

I slap his check back down onto the table. "Good to know."

Chapter
THIRTEEN

Monday after school, I sneak down past the football field to the recycling center. Abi sent me a text saying we needed to meet. Our normal meeting times are Friday mornings, when she hands off the payments, and Tuesday mornings, when she gives me the new client applications. What could be so important that it couldn't wait until tomorrow?

I find her pacing and mumbling to herself behind the last dumpster. Maybe she really is about to crack.

"What's up?"

I'm expecting her to announce for the hundredth time that she's quitting, but to my surprise, she shrugs. "Nothing's up. It's just … we received a few new applications, and I wanted to give them to you now instead of tomorrow."

"Okay. Because …?"

"No reason. Just didn't want to hang onto them.

Figured it might be better for you to look them over tonight at home, without having to face … never mind. Just take them." She avoids my eyes as she hands over the large manila envelope. I'm not sure which is shaking more, her voice or her hands. "I have to run and catch the bus."

She slips away behind the tree line and breaks into a jog toward the parking lot.

Oh, man. I think I know what this is about. One of those cheerleaders who was hanging all over Briggs the other night must want me to set them up.

Poor Abi. I know part of her still really cares for Briggsy. Even if it was her decision to break up, it can't be easy to watch someone else go after him.

I slump against one of the recycling dumpsters. What am I going to do? Only once have I ever turned away an applicant, and that was because she wanted to date a guy who was already seeing someone. I won't break up existing couples. That's a hard and fast policy, and it says so right on my website. Otherwise, I promise no reasonable application will be denied. And success is guaranteed.

I take a deep breath and tear open the envelope. The first two applications are simple enough—a girl with a small part in the spring musical pining after the leading man and a freshman tuba player with her eye on a junior marching band drummer. Typical stuff.

My heart pounds as I pull out the third application. I brace myself and flip over the sheet.

No. Oh, please, no.

Your Name: Lindsay LaRouche
Your BFTB (Boyfriend to Be): Chris Broder

Chapter
FOURTEEN

Dear Jolene:

Why on earth do you want to go out with Brendon anyway? He's kind of an idiot. Did you know he wipes his mouth with his sleeve? And he refers to his mother as his "old lady"? Who does that?

I hate to break it to you, but love's not really a thing. It's a chemical reaction—a bunch of pheromones colliding with hormones. Do you want to be a slave to your endocrine glands?

Research shows that the same endorphin that makes you feel like you're in love can be found in chocolate. Do yourself a favor: BUY

SOME HERSHEY'S KISSES. Less stress, less drama, and infinitely less heartache. Plus, they're delicious.

I slump back in my chair and pull my hands through my hair, adjusting and readjusting my ponytail. Crap. Crappity crap, crap, crap. Why does my life have to suck so bad?

I sigh and hit "delete."

Lindsay LaRouche could have any guy she wanted. Why in the name of all that is good and holy does it have to be Chris? And why did she have to hire me to set them up? I glare at the offending envelope lying on my desk and try to console myself: *Come on, Lexi, it's not all bad. This will be the easiest $125 you've ever made.*

Nope. Not feeling any better.

What would it be like with the two of them together? I picture them walking down the hall holding hands. Chris whispers something into Lindsay's ear, sending her into giggles. They stop at her locker, and Chris holds her books for her while she fools with her combination. Chris taps his left foot the way he always does when he's waiting, letting off nervous energy. As he hands her books back, Lindsay smiles up at him, and he leans down and—

"Lexi!" Dad calls from the kitchen. "Dinner's ready."

I shake my head and try to lose the visual. Before heading downstairs, I slip into the bathroom to splash some cool water on my face.

Dad made his specialty tonight—chicken stir-fry with jasmine rice. I usually devour his stir-fry, but tonight I have no appetite. I nibble at a snow pea and hope my parents won't notice.

"Tell us about your game," Mom says. "And how was Virginia Beach?"

I shrug. I so do not want to talk about it. Part of me wishes I could tell them what's going on with Chris and me—or more accurately, not going on—but that'll never happen. Mom and Dad aren't exactly touchy-feely types. I've never really had a heart-to-heart with them, or even a conversation about anything too personal. Unless, of course, you count having *the* talk with my mom in the sixth grade, also known as the most excruciating fifteen minutes of my life.

"What's the matter, Lexi?" Mom reaches over and feels my forehead. "You look rather pale. And your eyes are puffy."

"I'm fine. A little tired."

"We would have come down for the tournament if we could. You know that, don't you? I mean, Carol's my boss, so I couldn't miss—"

"What?" I shake my head. "Of course, Mom. That's not it."

"Then what?"

"I told you, it's nothing."

We eat in silence for a while, but I can feel them staring. Finally, my dad clears his throat. "We kept up with the scores online. You put up some nice stats. And a nice win."

"I did. We did."

"Did you meet with any scouts?" Mom asks.

Speaking of things I don't want to talk about. I shake

my head and stab my fork into a mini carrot.

"I see." Mom purses her lips. "Perhaps they didn't want to be too pushy. I mean, most of them have already contacted—"

"Saw an interesting article the other day." I mash the carrot into my rice. "Apparently more and more high school grads are opting out of college, or they're taking just a few courses—the ones they actually need to get the jobs they want. Some super entrepreneurial types are starting their own businesses straight out of high school."

"Interesting." Dad walks over to the stove for another helping. "Can't say I blame them."

"For real?" I look up at him and so does mom.

"Absolutely. College is so expensive these days. Who wants to be saddled with a huge mountain of student loan debt?"

"Well, that's true." Mom nods in agreement and flashes a huge smile. "Thank goodness we don't have to worry about that. You keep up with your basketball, Alexis, and we'll be fine. You're blessed, you know. Truly blessed."

I shove a fork full of rice into my mouth. Bless this mess.

Chapter
FIFTEEN

F Hall is empty, as usual, but I bend down and fake-tie my shoelace to listen for footsteps. Once I'm satisfied no one is coming, I slip into the janitor's closet.

Abi is sitting on a footstool playing with a strand of hair she's dyed turquoise.

"Pretty color." I try to sound perky, or at least normal. Or at least not like I wish the world would end tomorrow.

"Here's the thing." She stands and sticks her finger in my face. "I've been trying to quit this stupid job for at least a month now. We've had a great run, but as they say, all good things must come to an end. Let's call it a day, announce the end of Boyfriend Whisperer Enterprises, and move on."

"Abi, we've been through this—"

"Yes, we have. But now you want out, too. Admit it."

I narrow my eyes at her. "Why do you say that?"

"Oh, come on. I know a crush when I see one. And Lindsay LaRouche is a total La-Douche. Time to close up shop and throw away her stupid application."

Part of me is mortified that my crush on Chris has been so obvious, but a bigger part is touched that Abi wants to help. Still, I shake my head. I spent all night and all morning thinking about this, and I've made my decision. "I'm going to whisper him. For her."

"What?" Abi stomps one of her six-inch Espadrille wedges hard on the floor. "Are you insane? It's not worth it. For a hundred twenty-five dollars?"

"A hundred once I give you your cut," I remind her. "And yes, it's worth it. This is a business—my business. And my policy is to accept all reasonable applications. That's more important than any silly crush."

Abi shakes her head. "I can't believe you, Miss Love-Is-But-a-Whisper-Away. Give me a freaking break. I'm not going to let you do this."

"It's not up to you. I'm doing it. Whether you're in or out makes no difference. Conversation over."

She stares at me in silence for a moment and then shrugs. "Fine. Suit yourself. But you have a lot to learn about love." She storms out of the closet, slamming the door behind her.

I ease myself onto the step stool, blinking back the tears that have been threatening all day. Abi's right. This pain isn't worth $100, or any amount of money, really. But it's not about money. It's about Chris.

Over and over last night, I replayed in my mind the

way he acted around Lindsay in Virginia Beach. The stammering, the awkwardness. I've seen those symptoms in half the guys I've whispered. Chris likes Lindsay, plain and simple. He likes Lindsay and not me. He doesn't even think of me as a girl, for crying out loud. Am I happy about it? No. Is there anything I can do about it? Well, yes. I can set him up. Because it would make him happy. Because he's my friend, and that's what friends do.

At least, that's what I've been trying to convince myself. I bury my head in my hands and let the tears fall.

Chapter
SIXTEEN

I point to the strand of copper wire lying on the chem lab table in front of Chris. "That one's next."

As he hands it to me, our fingers touch briefly, and I feel a tingle of electricity. I glance sideways at him. Was it just me, or did he feel it, too? Copper is a strong conductor, after all. My gaze shifts across the room to Lindsay's table, and I remind myself that Chris is off limits now. Last night, I officially accepted the job of whispering him and emailed her my first set of instructions. She should be sauntering over here any minute to carry them out.

"I'm secretly hoping the coconut water has the most electrolytes," Chris says.

I blink. "What? You can't root for the coconut water. Our hypothesis is that the Gatorade will win."

He laughs. "It's not a contest, Lexi. It's an experiment."

He raises his voice. "And disproving a hypothesis is as valuable to scientific research as proving it, isn't that right Ms. Gupta?"

"That is correct, Christian. A hypothesis is an educated guess. There would be no point in conducting the experiment if there weren't a chance your guess could be wrong."

I raise my eyebrows at Chris. "Well, my hypothesis is that I'm going to double-check your results sheet to make sure you don't cheat."

"And my hypothesis is that you'd double check my results sheet anyway."

"Touché. Here, hold this for me." I hand Chris a pen cap and start wrapping the copper around it. "So now I'm going to triple-check them. The coconut water? Seriously? You're a traitor."

Chris shrugs. "I like coconut water better than Gatorade. So shoot me."

I aim my finger at him and pull the trigger.

"Whoa, am I interrupting something?" Lindsay appears at his side. "You look like you're ready to go evil on Chris's ass."

I assume she means medieval, but I refrain from correcting her and transform my scowl into a smile. "No, no. A mild flesh wound to the shoulder would suffice."

But Lindsay has already moved on and is ignoring me. She has her hand wrapped around Chris's bicep. "Can you help us with something? Allison and I are trying to figure out how to measure the pH of lemonade, but we can't figure out how to read the results."

Chris nods toward the pen cap still in his hand. "Um. Well, we're kind of in the middle of—"

"Go." I grab the cap from him. "It's fine. I've got this." I resist the urge to wink at Lindsay. Sometimes pretending I have no idea what's going on when in fact I've orchestrated the entire scene is the hardest part of being the Boyfriend Whisperer. I hate that Lindsay thinks I'm oblivious right now. Especially when this plan was such a stroke of genius.

I watch as she and Allison huddle on either side of Chris and explain their lemonade dilemma. My aborted email to Jolene the other night gave me the idea. The two of them are secretly testing whether wearing perfume with pheromones makes guys more attentive. Assuming they followed my instructions, Lindsay should be wearing the perfume and Allison should be wearing nothing more than a splash of lavender water.

As experiments go, it's horrible, actually, because Allison isn't the greatest control. She's plainer than Lindsay and a bit of a spaz. But, hey, I'm guaranteeing a boyfriend here, not a chem grade.

Whether to my satisfaction or dismay—I can't decide—the experiment appears to be working. Chris is leaning much closer to Lindsay as he explains how to read the litmus strips. Boy is brilliant at chemistry, and I have to say, listening to him talk about hydrogen ions over there is pretty sexy. Or would be if he weren't a mark for one of my clients, which he is. In fact, he appears to be a very willing mark, which means it's entirely possible that my goal of getting the two of them together in time for Valentine's, which is only four days away, is not entirely unrealistic, and isn't that a cheering thought?

My fingers reach the end of the wire, snapping me back to the task at hand. Shoot. I've wrapped way too much around this stupid pen cap.

"Is that what you want to do to me?" Chris slides back onto his stool and points to the tangle of wire as I begin unraveling it.

"What do you mean?"

"Strangle me? Listen, Lexi, if it makes you feel any better, I'm good either way. Coconut water or Gatorade. It's no big—"

"What? No. That's not it."

He looks from my face to the pen cap and back, clearly skeptical. "Then what?"

"It's … It's nothing. I read the instructions wrong; that's all. I thought I was supposed to wrap the whole thing around. Anyway, never mind me. What's up with those two?" I nod toward Lindsay and Allison.

Chris shrugs and lowers his voice. "No idea. Apparently, they're trying to measure the acidity of a bunch of different liquids, but when I asked them about it, neither of them could tell me what the point is or what they're trying to prove. I don't think they know what they're doing."

I steal another glance at Lindsay with her meticulously applied lipstick, her short-short jean skirt, and her too-tight top. She smiles, gives Chris a breezy wave, and mouths, "Thank you."

Au contraire, mon frère. That chick knows exactly what she's doing.

Chapter
SEVENTEEN

"Nice break." I size up the table and decide to take stripes. I bend down, pointing my cue stick at the nine-ball. "Left corner pocket."

Chris gives a low whistle. It's a high-risk shot, but I don't feel like playing it safe today. It's Saturday, and I've invited myself over to his house for the afternoon. I need to work fast if I'm going to set Lindsay and him up by Valentine's. He didn't stick around after chem to talk to her on Thursday and pretty much ignored her during class on Friday. I have no idea whether pheromone perfume actually works, but if it does, its effects on teen boys seem to be temporary. Time to grit my teeth and rip off this nasty Band-Aid.

I sink the nine-ball and head over to the other side of the table to attempt a bank shot on the twelve-ball. "Hard to believe it's mid-February already," I say.

"No way you make that shot."

"What?"

"The bank. It's too tight."

"Watch me."

He's right. I miss by a mile. Oh, well, it was worth a try. I step back and let him puzzle out how to tackle the solids. "So, like I was saying, hard to believe it's February twelfth already. Seems like New Year's was just yesterday."

Chris points his cue at the right side pocket. "Three-ball." He crouches down and assesses the angle. "Are you proposing what I think you're proposing?"

"Depends on what you think I'm proposing."

"*Chuck.* Time for another marathon."

I smile. We watched the first two seasons over New Year's. "Well, we do need to watch season three before I forget what happened, but that's not—"

The doorbell rings, causing Chris to pull up short on his shot and miss. "Dammit. If you win, this game will have an asterisk next to it."

"*When* I win." I check the clock on the microwave. Abi is right on time. While he runs upstairs to answer the door, I grab an iced tea out of the fridge and perch on a stool at the wet bar. *You've got this, Lexi. All is going according to plan. Hang in there.*

"What the—" Chris appears on the staircase carrying a tiny teddy bear dressed in a Bulls t-shirt and holding a bag of candy hearts. "Someone left this on the porch."

"Cute. What's the card say?"

He tears open the envelope. "To Chris. Happy

Valentine's from your Secret Admirer." He turns it around and around in his hands. "Weird."

The bear is way more obvious than my usual opening play, but (a) I'm trying to fast track this stupid thing, (b) Chris isn't into playing a bunch of head games, and (c) I'm thinking when it comes to crushes, the boy needs to be whacked over the head with a nine iron. Subtlety won't do.

"Who do you think it's from?" I ask.

"No idea."

"Oh, come on. You have to have some clue. Surely you've noticed someone acting differently around you lately? Flirting?" *Practically assaulting you on the couch in Virginia Beach? Hanging onto your every word in chemistry class?*

Chris shakes his head. "Not really."

"You're sure? Think about it."

He shrugs. "I mean, obviously, it could be any number of girls attracted to my incredible physique and boyish good looks, not to mention my charming personality."

"And your sense of modesty."

"That too." Chris laughs—a soft, sweet laugh that sends a thousand daggers through my heart. "Honestly, I have no idea who it could be."

"Well, Valentine's is Monday. You'd better figure it out quick."

He sets the bear next to me on the wet bar and steps back to admire it. "Whoever it is knows I like the Bulls. That's a good start."

"Must be someone special." My voice breaks, but I force a smile.

Chris sits down next to me. "What should I do now?"

"What do you mean?"

"I've never had a secret admirer. What am I supposed to do?"

"Well." I stroke the bear's ear. It's as soft as a cotton ball. "You should figure out who she is and do something nice for her. Bring her flowers or balloons or something on Monday."

"But what if it's someone I don't like?"

I hop down off the stool and walk over to the pool table. "What if it's someone you do? You don't want to miss your chance."

Love doesn't come around every day. My eyes cloud over as I stare down at the shiny black eight-ball. *I'm doing the right thing, aren't I? This is all going to work out fine?*

I could almost swear it answers me: *Signs point to heartache ahead.*

Chapter
EIGHTEEN

The fragrance of love permeates the halls Monday morning. Between the girls wearing fancy perfumes and the guys bearing bouquets, it's enough to make even the most cynical person smile. Or perhaps gag. Half of me wants to commandeer the school P.A. system and announce that I, Lexi Malloy, am to thank for most of these lovebirds' newfound bliss. The other half fantasizes about finding the world's largest bulldozer and flattening the whole freaking school with everyone in it. Love-schmov.

Even I have to admire the scene that plays out in second period study hall, though. Jolene happens to sit three rows to my left, and about five minutes after the bell, someone knocks on our classroom door. Mr. Ingersoll opens it to find a bald guy in a huge heart-shaped costume standing there.

"Singing telegram!" he says. Or rather, sings. He charges around Mr. Ingersoll and into the classroom, stopping at Jolene's desk. "Jolene Cinders?"

"Um. Yes?" Jolene looks as though she wishes the earth would open up and swallow her. The rest of the class is too astounded to say or do anything.

Heart dude gets down on one knee and places his hands over where … well, where the heart's heart would be, I guess, and starts to croon.

There is a young girl at Grand View
Who seems almost too good to be true.
Her taste in music and movies and fashion
Ignites in Brendon McDonough a passion
As no one else ever could do.

Yes, there is a young girl at Grand View
Whose smile could light up a room.
She's hot as a jalapeño.
So hot, it's insane, yo.
Tell me, what is a young man to do?

Oh, there is a young girl at Grand View
And Jolene, that young girl is you.
On this Feast of St. Valentine
Would you be ever so kind?
Please accept Brendon's love, pure and true.

Seemingly from nowhere, he pulls out a huge stuffed puppy with a pink candy heart sticking out of its mouth and hands it to a gaping Jolene.

Aww. The whole class bursts into applause. Some of the supposedly tough guys in the room look around at each other, but they must be too stunned to play rude. Or perhaps even they have been bitten by the Valentine's bug.

The whole thing is almost enough to make me reconsider my sour mood toward the ultimate Hallmark holiday. Almost.

Lindsay LaRouche's locker sits just around the corner from mine, which is good because every chance I get, I pass by, seeking a sign that Chris has taken my Boyfriend Whisperer bait. A balloon tied to the handle, a love note stuck in one of the vents, but there's nothing. A few times I catch Lindsay there, and she looks as miserable as though she just found out her favorite hair gel has been discontinued.

Maybe the secret admirer stunt was too subtle after all. Dammit. I really, truly, and seriously do not wish to spend the next three weeks trying to set the two of them up.

After the last bell, I grab my books and round the corner for one last check, hoping that maybe Chris was just playing it cool, waiting until the end of the day to make his move. That would be so Chris. But no, I find Lindsay alone and utterly Valentine-less, glaring into the recesses of her locker. I turn to leave before she catches me staring, only to run smack into someone's chest.

"Uh, hey, Lexi." Chris's face is as red as the dozen roses he's holding. It is perhaps the loveliest arrangement I have ever seen, right down to the baby's breath that seems to float among the blooms. Who knew the boy had such great taste in flowers?

"Hey there." I have to steady myself, whether because of the encounter with his chest, the perfume of the roses, or the realization that Operation Chris and Lindsay is finally about to go down, I'm not sure.

"So, I kind of um …" Chris swallows hard. "I mean, it took me a while, but I think I figured out who my secret admirer is."

"Yeah?" I struggle to keep my voice steady. "That's awesome. Pretty flowers, by the way."

"You like them?"

"Very much." I step aside. "I'm sure she will, too."

Chris tilts his head. "What do you—"

"Oh my gosh, those are amaaaazing." Lindsay appears beside me, arms outstretched. "Are they for me?"

Chris looks at me, so I force a smile, nod, and give him the thumbs-up. *Way to go. Now excuse me while I disappear to wallow in my pitiful, lonely, loveless existence.*

I turn and take off, hurtling down the hallway and through the front door without looking back. Yay, me. Another Boyfriend Whisperer Enterprises success story.

Chapter
NINETEEN

With the Valentine's rush over, Abi has no applications for me Tuesday morning, which is fortunate because I'm not in a matchmaking mood. Besides, I'll be swamped with basketball practice this week. We're headed to the state championship game on Saturday. It's kind of a big deal.

It's an A Day, so Chris and I share a lunch period. Ugh. I linger for a while outside the nurse's office contemplating how easy it would be to fake a stomachache, especially given the proximity of the stomach to the heart, but I know I can't avoid him forever. Might as well rip off another Band-Aid.

I skip the lunch line and grab a Power Bar from the machine. Somehow I don't think I can handle tacos today. When I get to our table, Chris and Massey are already there.

"So, have you banged her yet?" Massey is asking him.

Lovely. Simply lovely.

"Dude." Chris glances at me and his face darkens. "Show some respect. And what are you even talking about? We've been dating for exactly, what? Twenty-two hours?"

Twenty-one hours and ten minutes. Not that I'm counting.

Massey shakes his head. "Don't tell me you haven't noticed her …" He pauses to look at me and clears his throat. "Curves. Besides, rumor has it she's banged the entire soccer—"

"Shut up, Massey." I throw my half-eaten Power Bar at him. "You shouldn't be talking about girls like that. Especially not Chris's girlfriend." The cafeteria tilts slightly, and I grab the table to steady myself. I said it out loud. Chris has a girlfriend.

"Chill out, Lexi. What's your problem?" Massey picks up the Power Bar and takes a bite out of it before throwing it back at me.

I push my seat away, stand, and head for the door.

"Lexi! Lexi, wait!" Chris follows behind me. He catches up partway down the hall and grabs my arm. "Hold up."

I stop and face him.

"Don't let Massey bother you. He's an idiot."

"He's gross."

Chris's eyes hold an apology. "I'm not like that, you know."

"Like what?"

"What Massey was saying. I'm not like that. Shoot, Massey isn't even like that. He talks big."

Okay. This is awkward. I appreciate what Chris is trying

to do, but I really don't want to discuss his sex life, or even lack thereof. I look down at our feet, but that just makes me realize how gigantic his feet are, and then I start thinking about what they say about big feet, and … gaaahh, what the heck is wrong with me?

"I gotta run," I say, mostly to his feet. "I, um, have stuff to do."

"Lexi."

I look up.

"I feel like things are getting weird. Could we—"

"Hey there!" It's Lindsay. She's wearing a short, floaty purple dress and has one of the roses from yesterday's bouquet weaved into her hair. She strolls up to us and slips her arm through Chris's. "What's going on, you two?"

"Nothing." I shrink back a step. "We were talking. Obviously. About stuff. I mean … what's up with you?"

Lindsay shrugs. "Not much. You know, Chris, I was thinking. We should go to Lexi's game on Saturday. It's only about an hour away."

I hold my breath. Of course Chris is going to my game. It's the state championship. He sure as heck doesn't need her invitation.

He shifts from one foot to another. "Sure. Yeah, I was planning to, actually. We can go together."

"Sweet." Lindsay lifts her eyebrows at me. "I know you two are such great friends. This'll be fun."

I want nothing more than to yank that stupid rose out of her hair and stomp on it, but instead, I offer her a fist bump. "So fun."

Chapter
TWENTY

As horrible as it will be to see Chris and Lindsay together in the stands at the game Saturday, it's nothing compared to the torture of imagining what they're doing together Friday night.

They're out on their first date. Chris told me they were going to dinner at Ford's Fish Shack and the latest Bradley Cooper movie. Meanwhile, I'm sitting at home trying to keep myself occupied, earbuds cranked up to full blast, playing game after mind-numbing game of Angry Birds. I name every pig Lindsay.

Has he kissed her yet? *Blam.* Is he kissing her right now? *Blam.* Does he have his arm around her? Are they sharing popcorn? Are they going to sit all the way through to the end of the credits and make fun of the minor roles such as "Girl #3 in Bathroom Scene" like Chris and I always do?

Blam, blam, blam.

Partway through level four, my bedroom door flies open. "Lexi!" My mother looks ticked, sort of like Matilda just before one of her egg-shooting rampages.

I rip out my earbuds. "Don't you ever knock?"

"I did. Twice."

"What is it?"

She gives me her watch-your-tone glare. "I was just going through our shared files. You have some explaining to do."

Uh oh. Did I accidentally upload one of my Boyfriend Whisperer folders? Or maybe my financials? I take a deep breath and steady my voice. "What do you mean?"

"You know exactly what I mean." She steps into my room, hands on her hips. "You haven't updated your stats sheet in almost three weeks."

"Oh, right." I hope she can't hear the relief in my voice. "Sorry, Mom. I'll get to it this weekend." I point to my temple. "It's all up here."

Her eyes narrow. "I'm not so sure you have anything up there these days." She walks over and bends down to scrutinize me. "You're not doing drugs, are you?"

"What? No. Mom, it's a stupid spreadsheet. I'll take care of it."

She shakes her head. "Your stats are anything but stupid. Where do you think you'd be without them?"

I nod vaguely and say nothing. As soon as she shuts my door, I stick the earbuds back in and fire up another game. Where do I think I'd be without them? What's that supposed to mean? Where does *she* think I'd be without them?

Since my first basketball game in the sixth grade, I have scored exactly 543 points in regulation. That includes eighty-eight free throws, 184 two-point shots, and twenty-nine three-pointers. I know this because of my stats sheet—an Excel spreadsheet I'm supposed to update after every game. It automatically calculates my shot percentages, my year-over-year improvements, and the differential between my actuals and my goals.

Without it, where would I be?

Chapter
TWENTY-ONE

One bounce. Two bounces. Three. Bend the knees and close the eyes. Open the eyes, bounce the ball one more time, and shoot.

Swish.

Thank goodness. I have the highest free-throw percentage in Loudoun County and the second-highest in the state of Virginia, but we're only eight minutes into Saturday's game, and already I've missed two. About time I hit one.

Keisha gives me a fist bump as we race down to the other end of the court. "You good, Lex?"

I nod. "Caffeine's starting to kick in."

She laughs and shakes her head. "You're a trip."

Energy's not my problem. Focus is. I'm trying to keep my mind in the game, but it insists on wandering over to the bleachers. I'm a boss at ignoring the crowd—when you have parents like mine, that's crucial—but today I can't help but peer over every thirty seconds to check on Chris and Lindsay.

It's not a pretty sight. She's gripping his arm like a spider wrapping up its prey. Somehow her plastic giggle manages to rise above the shouts of the entire freaking crowd, even my parents. The way she gazes at Chris, the way she flings her hair into his chest, I can tell they've kissed. They've definitely kissed.

Whack. A forward from the other team slams into my left shoulder and passes me on her way to the basket.

"Malloy! What was that?" Coach calls a time out. Before I even reach the sidelines, she's in my face, blasting me for giving up the shot. "Take a seat."

I bite my lip. I've never been benched like this, not in the middle of a close game and certainly not with the state championship on the line. Fortunately, my parents are now sitting behind me, so I don't have to see the expressions on their faces.

I cheer as Carmella scores a lay-up, but after that, it's turnover after turnover and the other team goes up by two points, four points, seven points. *Okay, Reilly, put me in. You've made your point.*

Coach ignores me as she paces back and forth in front of my seat. Fine. I deserve it. I sucked out there, but is she seriously going to give up state?

Across the court, the other team's fans smell blood. They begin chanting. "Spar-tans! Spar-tans! Spar-tans!"

I look back at Lindsay and Chris to find her running

her hands through his hair. My stomach twists. I can tell she's teasing him because his face is bright red. Must be asking about the cowlick. I get that. It's so adorable. My fingers have itched to touch it many, many times over the past few months.

I risk a glance at my parents, who are sitting stone-faced and still. For years I'd have given anything for them to sit and watch my games quietly, but now their silence seems somehow louder than their shouting ever did.

Keisha scores two free throws, but then one of the Spartan guards immediately takes the ball down the court and sinks a three-pointer, making the score 23-15. If we don't turn things around soon, it'll be over. I stand up in the hopes that Coach will give up this stupid life lesson crap and put me in, but she never even acknowledges me.

Tears spring to my eyes. For real? I'm going to start crying? Maybe Coach and Chris and my mom are right. Maybe something is wrong with me. There's no crying in basketball. It's just … I'm not sure what to do, how to act.

For the past six years, I've started every game I've ever played. Off season, I've attended basketball camps every summer and practice clinics every fall. When not playing organized ball, I've spent half my free time on the courts at the park. Always trying to perfect my free throw, increase the range of my outside shot, take my layup a little higher.

Basketball isn't a game I play; it's who I am.

Or at least, it's who I used to be.

Chapter
TWENTY-TWO

"Good game. Good game. Good game." I walk down the line and slap the hand of each Spartan, struggling to keep a smile on my face. We lost by two points. Coach benched me for almost six minutes of game time. Had she put me in thirty seconds earlier, things could have been different.

"Lexi!" It's Chris, with Lindsay close behind. He gives me a hug. He doesn't say "great game" or "you tried your best" or "there's always next year." He knows. I don't need meaningless platitudes, just a hug.

Lindsay, on the other hand, does not know. "Wow, that was a close one," she says, her eyes wide with something resembling pity. "You must be devastated, especially since you were on the sidelines for so long. Still, second place is pretty good."

Second place is pretty good? And she calls herself a cheerleader? I search the crowd for my parents. This has to be the first time ever I've wanted to see them after a loss. Anything to get away from these two.

"Hey, we're stopping at Joe's Crab Shack for dinner on the way back. Why don't you come with?" Lindsay's hands are back to clutching Chris's biceps. Those nails have to be fakes. No one could grow nails that perfect.

"Thanks, but I—"

"Come on, Lex," Chris says. "It'll be fun. No ball talk, promise. And I hear they're running their crab cake special."

I consider this. I do love Joe's crab cakes. And basically, my choices are to ride back with them or with two very disappointed parents. Because no way am I getting on a bus full of girls who no doubt blame me for the fact that we lost and who will revel in the drama of my inglorious benching the entire way home. I'm debating my options when I spot my dad through the sea of celebrating Spartan fans. Woah. If looks could kill, Coach Reilly would be dead, cremated, and scattered across center court. "Wait here a minute," I call over my shoulder to Chris and Lindsay as I sprint to intercept him.

I block his warpath. "Hey, Dad. What's up?"

"What was that?" He points toward Coach. "What did she think she was doing?"

I'm tempted to commiserate. At least he's not mad at me. But my desire to avoid a scene outweighs my instinct to deflect his wrath. "Dad, it's no biggie. She benched me for a few minutes, and I deserved it. I wasn't getting it done out there. You saw me."

"What I saw was her best player struggling. You don't bench someone for that. You let her play through it. She cost Grand View the championship."

By now people are starting to stare. "Seriously, it's okay. And I wasn't struggling, I was … distracted."

"Distracted?" My mom has joined us, and she looks as though I've just announced that I am in fact doing drugs. "What on earth by?"

"I don't know. Life." I glance over to see Chris and Lindsay watching us, and all of a sudden playing third wheel at their Flirt Fest doesn't seem so bad. "Can't we save this conversation for later? I'm going to dinner with some friends, and then I'll be home. Let's talk about it then."

"No, this cannot wait." Mom folds her arms across her chest and juts her hip out. "Something is going on with you, Alexis, and I want to know what it is. Now."

I close my eyes. Where should I start? With the fact that I'm in love with my best friend? Or that I've managed to set him up with someone else? Or maybe I should lead off with the revelation that I no longer want to be the girl whose greatest achievement in life is that she can put a ball through a hoop better than all the other girls. That maybe there are other things I want to do, can do, and might even be good at doing.

I search the court for Coach Reilly, who is nowhere to be found. Good. She must have escaped to the locker room, unaware of the storm she just avoided. I lean in toward my mother and lower my voice. "I won't do this here, Mom. Maybe later." Without waiting for her response, I head over to Chris and Lindsay. "I'm in. Give me twenty minutes to shower, and I'll meet you in the parking lot."

Chapter
TWENTY-THREE

Sitting in the back seat of Chris's Corolla feels wrong in so many ways. For one thing, the seats are really short and low back here. Chris, of course, has to put his driver's seat all the way back, so I'm stuck behind Lindsay, who is sitting in my usual spot but is doing it all wrong. She keeps adjusting the heat and the music and the recline lever on her seat, and *doesn't she know everything was perfect before she came along and starting messing with it?*

Chris seems not the least bit annoyed by her constant "improvements," nor by her inane monologue on the benefits of acai juice, nor by the fact that she laughs just a little too long and too loud at his jokes, including sometimes when he's not even joking. By the time we reach the Shack, I'm starting to wonder whether an evening with my parents wouldn't have been the lesser of the two evils.

The hostess shows us to a booth near the back. I expect Lindsay to order a salad or perhaps the chicken fingers, but she surprises me and goes for the Alaskan crab legs. Messy. And potentially hell on her nails. As our server walks away, Lindsay turns to me. "I'm so glad you joined us, Lexi. Isn't this place fun?" She has to shout because half the wait staff have formed a dance posse and are kicking it up to *Cotton Eye Joe*. The crowd cheers them on, and two little girls at the table next to us get up and show off their moves.

Crap. This has always been my favorite restaurant in the world. I just know Lindsay's going to ruin it. I force a smile. "Love it."

Halfway through the song, one of the little girls walks over to Chris. She can't be more than eight years old. "Want me to show you how to do the Cotton Eye Joe?"

Girl's got guts. And excellent taste in boys. Unfortunately, she's about to get her heart crushed because Chris doesn't dance, ever. Sure enough, he smiles and shakes his head. "Thank you, but I'll just mess it up. You and your friend are really good at it, though."

She grins. "Thanks."

Lindsay leans forward and slaps the table. "I'll dance with you."

The girl's eyes light up as she grabs Lindsay's hand and pulls her out onto the dance floor. Lindsay, of course, doesn't miss a step. Perhaps learning cheer routines is an underrated skill.

I turn to Chris. "Why do you think she asked me to come out to dinner with you tonight? Doesn't it seem a little weird?"

"Weird?"

"Yeah. Two's company, three's a crowd, and all that." What I want to say is that if he and I were dating, I most certainly would not want anyone else along. I would want him all to myself, all night long. His eyes. His lips. His arms circling me and pulling me close to him until—

I blink hard. I have to stop doing that. Not only does Chris not think of me that way, he is now seeing someone. Time to get used to it. "I find it strange; that's all."

Chris shrugs and glances over at Lindsay, who is giving the little girl a fist bump mid-dance turn. "Maybe it's because she's a nice person and would like to be friends if you'll give her a chance."

I look away and take a sip of my lemonade. Well, well. Five days into their relationship and Chris is already taking Lindsay's side. Worst part is, he's right. She's been nothing but sweet to me all week and in fact has never been rude or unkind in the three years we've gone to school together. She's mostly ignored me, but then again, I've ignored her, too.

Lindsay bounces back into the booth. "Wow, that was fun. Though now I'm a sweaty mess." She has not a single drop of sweat on her, not even the slightest glistening across her forehead. Pretty sure I'm sweating more than she is from my mini-fantasy about Chris's hug. She takes a sip of her water. "I'm going to run to the restroom. If our waiter comes by, could you ask him to bring me a cranberry juice?" And with that, she takes off again.

I'm tempted to make a crack about whether she'd prefer acai juice but think better of it. Then, because I feel bad and because I know Chris had a point about her trying to be friendly, I decide to play nice. "She's a great dancer. And seems good with kids."

Chris shifts in his seat but says nothing.

I take a deep breath. "Anyway, I'm glad she did ask me to come out tonight. Riding home with Mark and Bev would've been a nightmare. Thanks for letting me tag along."

"First off, you're not tagging along. You're hanging out with us. Or we're hanging out with you. I mean … we're all hanging out together. And second, sorry about your parents. You know it's only because they have an unhealthy obsession with the sport, right?"

I laugh. If anyone else dissed my parents, I'd be pissed. Well, embarrassed and pissed. But Chris is allowed. He loves them, and they love him, almost like the son they never had.

The rest of the evening isn't horrible. Lindsay dominates the conversation with a rambling story about her stepsister who auditioned last season for a spot on "The Bachelor," but it's actually pretty funny. Who knew crowds of guys pooled in the parking lot in the hopes of hooking up with the contestant wannabes?

Somehow, Lindsay manages to pick apart her crab legs neatly and daintily and without a single casualty to her nails. Impressive. We're about to ask for the check when a line of wait staff files out of the kitchen. They march past the dance floor and down the aisle, straight to our booth.

"We understand someone has a birthday today," a tall guy shouts out to the entire restaurant. He's staring at Chris.

Lindsay kicks me under the table and winks, a mischievous smile playing on her lips.

No. She. Didn't.

One of the waitresses holds out a huge multi-colored afro wig. Chris's face matches the streak of pink running down the center of it. Oh, dear Lord. This should be interesting. On Chris's eleventh birthday he about died of embarrassment because his mom made him wear one of those little birthday-hat cones while we sang to him. And that was in the privacy of his own kitchen.

Chris turns to Lindsay as he tugs the 'fro onto his head. "I'm going to kill you."

The tall guy pulls up a chair from a nearby table. "And now, we need you to hop up here so we can sing 'Happy Birthday' to you."

"Tell you what," Chris says. "I think I'm tall enough." He gets to his feet, dwarfing everyone.

Tall Guy's eyes widen, and he pushes the chair back. "Alright-y, then." He looks around at the rest of the servers. "Ready?"

"Actually, I have a better idea." One of the waitresses steps forward and holds up a microphone. "How about if Chris sings 'Happy Birthday' to himself?"

Oh, my. If there is one thing Chris is even less likely to do in public than dance, it's sing. No way will he go for this. Lindsay's joke was cute, but it's over. Chris is going to pull out his license and prove to everyone that today is not, in fact, his birthday.

Only he doesn't. He takes the mic, strolls down the aisle to the dance area and strikes a rock star pose. He mock head-bangs to the point that tufts of the wig start to fall off and belts out the most overly dramatic version of the birthday song ever performed. The crowd, as they say, goes wild, while I sit in stunned silence. Because first of all, the boy's got pipes. He can sing. And second of all, what the what?

As the applause subsides, Chris hands the mic back to the waitress and returns to our booth.

"What was that?" I point to the dance floor. "Since when do you know how to sing?"

He shrugs. "I sing in the shower."

"Okay, but …" I force myself past the visual. "Why have I never heard you before? Like, not even in the car. You're good."

"Oh, come on. It was 'Happy Birthday.'"

"It was awesome."

"Yes, it was." Lindsay wraps one hand around his neck and pulls him toward her. "Time for your birthday kiss."

Ugh. The kiss lasts approximately four hours, or maybe four seconds, I can't be sure. I try to look away, but I can't. My stomach twists, sending pangs of regret coursing through me—regret for having eaten that second crab cake, regret for coming here tonight, and most of all, regret for setting the two of them up in the first place. Why did I do that again?

Chris finally pulls away from Lindsay. His face is bright red, but he's wearing a goofy grin, and I remind myself: *That's why. Chris is happy. And he deserves to be happy. And as his best friend, I am happy to see him happy.*

He stands and grabs his coat off the hook beside our

booth. "Let's split before they decide to do the Macarena and make me join in. I was here one time when they picked on the birthday girl the entire night."

Fine with me. Lindsay and I grab our coats and follow him out to the car. I barely notice Lindsay's fidgeting on the way home. I'm too busy reminding myself of how happy I am.

Chapter
TWENTY-FOUR

My parents are not happy. They're waiting for me in the den when I get home. My dad has kicked back in his recliner, his display case looming behind him. The wall-length monument to his brief career is crammed with photos, news clippings, trophies, game balls, and jerseys.

Chris and I used to stand for what seemed like hours admiring everything in the case. My favorite piece has always been the *Washington Post* photo of Dad shooting a championship game buzzer beater in his Wheaton High uniform. He looks so young. Chris's favorite is the basketball signed by Michael Jordan, one of the greatest players in the history of the Bulls.

Once when we were about nine, I dared him to take the Jordan ball out. I knew where my dad kept the keys to the case, though I'd never worked up the nerve to open it.

Chris took the dare. His eyes shone as he held the ball, his finger tracing the huge loop of the "J" in his idol's last name.

But then my mom caught him. "Christian Broder!" She stood in the doorway of the den, eyes ablaze.

Chris froze. "I … I'm …"

I stepped forward. "It's my fault, Mom. I dared him."

"Oh, don't you worry, young lady. You're in trouble, too." Mom turned back to Chris.

"No, Mrs. Malloy." He found his voice. "Lexi tried to stop me. She shouldn't get in trouble."

I still did, of course—no TV for a week—but Chris had it worse. His parents grounded him from TV, the computer, and video games for two weeks. I thought he'd be mad, but when I saw him in school the next day, he thanked me. "It's M.J., Lexi. M.J."

Chris wanted to grow up to be just like Michael Jordan. Even now, at seventeen, though he has a more realistic view of his chances, he still wants to take his basketball career as far as he can. He loves the game, and he'd play forever if he could.

Me, on the other hand? Not so much. And somehow I need to break the news to my parents. Maybe tonight's the night, with my junior-year season behind me and my entire senior year ahead. It's not that I don't want to play next year. I do. But if I make it clear that basketball is not my entire future, my meal ticket, maybe next year doesn't have to be so intense.

I take a deep breath and sit down on the couch next to my mom.

"How was Joe's?" she asks.

Small talk—a good sign that they're not totally pissed at me. "It was fine. I got the crab cakes."

Mom glances at my father. "We think we know what this is about. Your … distraction."

Aaaand … thus ends the small talk. My jaw tenses. I have no idea what their theory is, but it's wrong. Or partially right at best. Because when I said I was distracted by life, I meant it. There's no one simple explanation.

"This is about a boy, isn't it?" The corners of Mom's lips curl up in a half smile.

Oh, jeez. Okay, part right.

"Sweetheart." Dad places his elbows on the arms of his chair and brings his massive hands together, his fingers forming a church and a steeple, like the game he used to play with me when I was little. "We know you're growing up. Sometimes faster than we'd like." His eyebrow twitches, and my mom fidgets next to me.

Oh, no. I flash back to the sixth grade. Please tell me we are not having the growing up and liking boys and protecting my virtue talk.

Dad continues. "But there will be plenty of time for boys after college."

I blink. College? They expect me to place my love life on hold for another five years?

"That's right." Mom chimes in. "Right now, boys are exactly what you said—a distraction. One you can ill afford. Do you know, I was reviewing your stats sheets this evening, and while the number of three-pointers you made this year went up from last year, the percentage actually went down?"

She reveals this in the same pained tone I imagine her using when she breaks it to her boss that their company's profit margins have dropped. I remember her explaining to my dad once that for every one percent decrease in annual profits, the company had to cut twelve staff.

But come on. My three-point shots are hardly a life-and-death matter. And why should the fact that I sat out a game for six minutes—well, five minutes and fifty-six seconds, not that I was counting—trigger a freaking all-out red alert? It's a *game*, people.

I clasp my hands together and stare down at them. How many times over the years have I wanted to shout that very sentence to my parents? Every time Dad's bellow echoed across the court when the ref made a bad call, every time Mom nagged me about updating my stats sheet, every time we drove home from a loss in deafening silence.

I look up at my dad. "First of all, I'm not waiting to date until after college. That's preposterous. Second of all ..."

Dad grimaces and rubs his bad knee. I force myself not to roll my eyes. *I get it, Dad. You blew out your knee and your career, and now you want me to pick up where you left off. Can you spell 'cliché'?*

"Second of all, this isn't about a boy. At least, not entirely. I happen to have a lot going on right now. Basketball is just one part of my life, you know."

"Darling, of course we know that." Mom pats my leg. "You have your schoolwork, and that's important. And you want to hang out with your friends. Perfectly normal. But—"

"But what? You two have drilled it into my head since

I was six years old that I should be a well-rounded player—someone who could pass, dribble, catch, shoot, block. Maybe I want to be a well-rounded human being, too. Basketball is only one piece of my life. And it may not even be the most important piece."

"What?" My mother's mouth twists. "Where is this coming from, Alexis? You've worked too hard to get where you are to treat basketball like a … a hobby."

"That's the problem. It's become work. As in, not a game. Not fun. I can't tell you how psyched I am that this season is over."

"So what are you trying to say?" Dad's still rubbing his knee. "You don't want to do camp this year? Is that it? Because we can take a summer off from camp and concentrate on your physical training if you want."

"Physical training. Because that's a blast." I shake my head. Time to spit this out. Pull off one more Band-Aid. "What I'm trying to say is …"

But I can't do it, because something in my dad's eyes is begging me not to break his heart. I can see in his expression all the hours he's logged doing passing and shooting drills with me, all the miles he's driven for my practices, tournaments, and camps, and all the scraped knees and elbows he's helped make all better.

I sigh. "I need a break; that's all. I'm burnt out. Just give me some time."

Who knows? Maybe a little time is all I need.

Chapter
TWENTY-FIVE

A noise startles me, and I turn to see the garage door closing. Oh, no. For a moment I consider dashing over, dropping, and rolling beneath it in a dramatic escape, but after all, I'm a basketball player, not a gymnast. With my luck, one of my limbs would get stuck and have to be amputated.

I'm researching Nick Garland for a client, and now I'm stuck in his garage. Lovely. What if he walks in and finds me? What possible excuse could I give for sneaking in here? This is the end. I'm totally going to be outed. Everyone will find out I'm the Boyfriend—

Oh, gosh. What if his mom or dad finds me? Forget being outed. I could go to jail for trespassing. That's what it would be, right? I mean, it wouldn't be breaking and entering because technically I didn't break anything to get in. The garage door was wide open when I snuck into his yard. Maybe if my parents get me a good lawyer I could plead my way to community service or—

I shake my head and blink hard. *Chill, Lexi. Think. There has to be a way out of this.* I tiptoe to the inside door and slowly, gently turn the knob. It gives. Good. So it's not locked. Of course, I can't exactly saunter into the Garlands' mudroom or kitchen or wherever the heck this door leads, but at least I'm not completely trapped. I take out my phone and dial Abi. *Pick up. Please, please, please pick up.*

"Hello?"

"Abi! I need a favor."

"Lexi? I can barely hear you."

"I'm whispering."

"What?"

"I'm— Never mind. I need a favor."

There's a pause, and I can feel Abi rolling her eyes. I always need a favor.

"You always need a favor."

"I know, and I'm sorry, but this time, it's serious. And … immediate."

Another pause. "What is it?"

"I'm in Nick Garland's garage, and I need you to help me get out."

"What? Why?"

"Because I don't want to go to jail."

"No, I mean, why are you in his garage?"

"I wanted to gather some intel, though frankly it's been a total waste of my time. He has some motor cross stuff, a bunch of hunting paraphernalia—exactly what you'd expect for a guy who wears flannel every day to school. Anyway, apparently somebody somewhere hit a button and … well, I'm trapped. I need your help."

There's a long pause on the other end of the line. Finally, Abi replies. "What exactly am I supposed to do?"

I smile. Abi always comes through. "It's no big deal. I just need you to come over here and create a distraction—something that will get everyone out of the house."

"A distraction? How am I—"

"You've got this, Abi. You can do it." I hang up and press my ear against the door. Somewhere inside a television is on. I can hear singing. It sounds like some sort of cartoon. I squeeze my eyes shut and concentrate. It sounds so familiar but … oh, my. No way. Is that *My Little Pony*? Could Nick be a Brony? Mr. Mountain Boots and Two-Inch Beard? Or maybe he has a kid sister.

I crack the door open the teeniest bit. He's rustling around in the next room, which must be the kitchen because I can hear cabinet doors opening and closing and the sound of silverware clanging. The smell of peanut butter makes my mouth water. And that's when he starts humming. I bite my lip to keep from laughing. He *is* a Brony. Nick Garland. Of all the things I love about being the Boyfriend Whisperer, this is definitely at the top of the list. I learn something new every day about my classmates. People are rarely exactly as they seem.

Soon after Nick finishes making his snack and goes back into the TV room, the doorbell rings. Show time. I hear footsteps and the front door opening. I crack the door wider to listen.

"Hey."

"Hi. It's Nick, right?"

"Yeah."

"I'm Abi. We go to school together."

"I know." Nick sounds confused. And wary.

"Can you help me? I think there's a snake in my car."

I clamp my hand over my mouth to keep from laughing. A snake? In her car? I love Abi.

"There I was, driving innocently down the road, when all of a sudden I saw this little head peek out from under the passenger seat." Abi sounds appropriately hysterical. "Of course, I pulled over immediately and, well, thank goodness you're someone I know. This would be so embarrassing if … by the way, is anyone else home?"

"My mom's upstairs."

"Could she help too?"

"What?"

"It would be great if she could help. There's safety in numbers, you know."

"She's taking a nap." It's apparent from Nick's tone that he thinks Abi is insane.

"I see. Well, I guess that's okay."

"It's okay if my mom takes a nap?"

"I guess. I mean, of course it is. What about your sister?"

"What?"

"Your—"

"Oh, that." The television goes mute. "Right. Yeah, that's … it's not what … I mean, she just left."

"Ah. Okay. Anyway, that's my car over there. The red

one across the street. Let's go get that snake." She practically shouts the last sentence, no doubt for my benefit, though I'm hoping it wasn't also loud enough to wake Mrs. Garland.

I take a deep breath and step into what turns out to be a laundry room when I hear the front door open again and Nick's voice. "I have some nets in the garage. Let me grab one."

"No, no. I don't think that'll be necessary." Abi sounds panicked. "How about if we just open all the doors and I'll hit my car alarm and—"

"Give me one minute."

Oh, no. I slip back into the garage and crouch down behind a huge pile of fishing gear. Which, I realize too late, includes several nets. I curl into as tight a ball as possible and tuck in my chin. I am so busted.

Sure enough, Nick walks straight over to the fishing nets. I hold my breath.

It takes him a solid three minutes to untangle the net he wants. The entire time he's muttering, wondering how someone manages to wind up with a snake in her car. At last, he frees the net with one final pull, which sends one of the rods crashing into my forehead. It stings like crazy, but I manage to hold in my yelp.

Finally, he turns and leaves, and I hear the front door open and close. I waste no time slipping through the laundry room and into the kitchen toward the back door. I make it halfway to the door when I hear footsteps on the staircase.

"Nick?" It's his mom. "Did I hear a doorbell?"

Ugh. There's no turning back. I make a run for the

door, knowing she'll hear it slam behind me. I just hope I can make it across her yard and down the street before she catches me. Except at the exact moment I reach the door, Abi's car alarm goes off. It's loud enough to hide the slamming door. Heck, it would be loud enough to hide the sound of a freight train running through their house. Once again, Abi to the rescue.

As I race through the neighbors' yards, I shoot her a text.

Lexi: I owe you big time. Meet me at my house once you've gotten rid of that snake.

Chapter
TWENTY-SIX

I circle back around through Nick's neighborhood to retrieve my car, stop by Starbucks for two mocha lattes, and pull up to my house to find Abi waiting for me on the front porch.

"What are you doing?" I hiss at her. "What if someone from school were to drive by and see you sitting here? Quick, get inside."

"You're welcome." She stands and follows me into the den. "No, really. It's no problem. Just because I'll be up until two in the morning finishing my history essay on the fall of the Berlin Wall doesn't mean you have to act grateful."

"Sorry." I hand her one of the lattes. "I am grateful. It's just that I've been freaked out enough about being outed this afternoon. If Nick had caught me ... you were brilliant, by the way."

Abi sinks onto a recliner and sips at her coffee. "Would that really be so bad?"

"What? If he'd caught me?" I shudder at the thought. "Do you know he was standing three feet away when he came to get that net? I don't know how he missed me."

"I mean being outed, being known as the Boyfriend Whisperer. There are some happy couples out there who might want to thank you."

I roll my eyes. "Abi, we've been through this before. Not an option." First of all, if people knew my identity, it would make my job harder. Second, my guy friends would never let me live it down. Most of them think the whole concept of the Boyfriend Whisperer is absurd. Of course, some of those same guys have unwittingly been whispered, so that shows how much they know. But now, most important, is Chris. I'm pretty sure he'd be pissed to find out he's been whispered and even more pissed to know it was by me.

Abi scoots forward in the recliner. "It must be killing you."

"What?"

"Chris and Lindsay. They're so … kissy face together. It even bugs me."

It's true. They're the ultimate insta-couple. They've been together less than two weeks, but it's like they're practically married. The worst is at lunch. Lindsay eats with us every A Day now and completely monopolizes the conversation, not to mention the fact that she touches Chris an average of 253.5 times a minute.

Part of me wants to break down and cry right here in front of Abi. Instead, I plaster on the fake smile that has become my go-to expression. "He's happy. She's happy. That's what Boyfriend Whisperer Enterprises is all about."

Abi rolls her eyes. "Earth to Lexi. Boyfriend Whisperer Enterprises is a product of your imagination."

"And hard work."

"Okay, and hard work. But that means it can be whatever you want it to be. Or it can … not be at all. Wait, wait, wait. Hear me out." She holds up her hands to shush the protest she knows is coming. "Think about this. Nothing lasts forever, especially not high school stuff. That's what college is for—so we can get away from all the messes we've created. You're always talking about people taking charge of their own destiny. Why not take charge of your destiny and shut BFW down now? Go out while you're on top?"

"I can't."

Abi sighs. "I try."

I scoot forward and set down my coffee, my voice low. "I need to tell you something. Can you keep a secret?"

She narrows her eyes and purses her lips.

"Right. Sorry. Of course you can." I shake my head in an apology. "Okay." Another deep breath. "I'm not planning to shut it down. Not this year, not next year … maybe never."

Abi's eyebrows creep up. "Um, Lexi, I hate to break it to you, but your grades are way too high for this plan to work. Unless you plan to purposely flunk senior year in perpetuity?"

"Perpetuity? Nice word."

She sticks out her tongue. "I'm more than just a pretty face."

"I never said you were a pretty face. I mean, obviously, you have a pretty face, but I know you're smart. Anyway. The Boyfriend Whisperer. I want to keep it going even after I'm gone. After I graduate. I was thinking about going to NoVa part-time to take some business courses and some web courses so I can turn the Boyfriend Whisperer into a franchise. I'll start with Loudoun County schools, but eventually, I want it to go nationwide—a BFW in every high school in the country."

"Whoa." Abi waves her hands in the air. "Back up. First of all, NoVa? As in, community college? Lexi, I'm not one to diss community college, but, hello? They don't have basketball. What are you even talking about?"

I close my eyes. This is a conversation I'll have to have many times over the next fifteen months if I want to make my plan a reality. "I know it sounds weird, and I know I'm going to sound like an ungrateful brat, but I don't think I want to play college ball."

"What?"

"Don't get me wrong. I love the game. I'd miss it. I'd probably think about coaching at the Y or something like that, but I'm just ... over it."

"What do you mean, over it?"

"The pressure, the team drama, the stats. I don't want four more years of it."

"But ... wow." Abi slumps back into her chair and lets out a low whistle. "Have you told your parents?"

I quirk an eyebrow at her.

"Guess not. Holy cow. So not Coach, or Chris, or anyone?"

"Abi, no one else knows about the Boyfriend Whisperer. How could I?"

"Right. So how will you?"

"I don't know. I figure I have at least until the fall to figure that out. At that point, the colleges are going to start getting super pushy. Anyway, what do you think? Can I pull it off?"

"You? Hells yeah, if anyone can. But are you sure you want to? Don't you get tired of all the hassle and secrecy and … what is that bruise on your forehead?"

I dab at the tender spot where Nick Garland's fishing rod whacked me. "Occupational hazard. And no, I don't get tired of it. It's fun coaching my clients. And if I franchise the businesses, I'll get to coach all my franchisees on how to do the same thing for their clients. How cool is that?"

Abi looks doubtful, but she nods. "If that's what you want, I'll support you. Or at least cheer you on. With my pretty cheerleader face."

I laugh and give her a fist bump. "Thank you. That actually means a lot to me. Now, tell me. What's going on with you and Briggsy?"

"Ugh. Briggs." Abi sighs, and her eyes grow misty, as they tend to do when the conversation turns to her ex. "Nothing's going on. We're done. I've moved on."

The catch in her voice tells me she most definitely has not moved on. "Listen, Abi, I'm not one to say a girl needs a boyfriend. And you of all people can get along just fine without Briggsy or anyone else. You're smart, strong, resourceful … who else would have thought to tell Nick Garland she had a snake in her car? But it's obvious you miss Briggs. And he misses you, too."

Abi trains her eyes on mine. "Did he say something?"

I look away and say nothing. Discretion. Even when it's Abi.

"Whatever. Like I said, we're done. I may miss him, but I don't miss watching him flirt with other girls when he's supposed to be with me. At least now when I see him flirting, it's simple jealousy and not humiliation." Abi sniffles, and I give her a sympathetic smile.

She's right, of course. Briggs is an insatiable flirt. The thing is, I honestly believe he doesn't mean to be. He's just naturally charming and funny and outgoing. I don't think he even knows how to dial it back. I suppose that can be tough on a girlfriend.

Abi's phone buzzes. She checks her text and frowns. "Anita Alvarez. She's our third applicant in the past twenty-four hours."

I sigh. "Guess it's officially prom season."

"Yippee." Abi takes a sip of her latte.

What can I say to cheer her up? I give her a conspiratorial grin. "So, about Nick's little sister …"

Her eyes grow wide. "He doesn't have one, does he?"

"I don't think so."

We both melt into giggles.

"Oh my gosh," she says. "That is so awesome. Nick Garland. Who would have thought?"

"I know, right? With the flannel shirts and the pickup truck."

"And the bumper sticker that says, 'I love animals. They're delicious.'" Abi squeals. "We should get him a *My*

Little Pony bumper sticker."

"Ah, ah, ah." I shake my finger at her. "What's the word?"

She rolls her eyes and pouts. "I know. Mum."

"Exactly. No one can know."

"Whatever." Abi sits up, her face suddenly serious. "So do you think he's more of a Twilight Sparkle guy? Or Rainbow Dash?"

We both lose it all over again.

Chapter
TWENTY-SEVEN

I jab Chris hard with an elbow to the side and take the shot.
    "What was that?" He bends over and rubs the spot
where I semi-impaled him.

"You were crowding the basket. What was I supposed
to do?"

It's the first Saturday morning in March, and it's a
gorgeous day—sunny and crisp. I've challenged Chris to
a game of one-on-one because I wanted to do something
with just the two of us, like old times. Like up until twelve
days ago, not that I'm counting. Except this is nothing like
old times, because all I can think about is the fact that *Chris
has a girlfriend.*

"Let's take a break." He pulls a small towel out of his
waistband and strolls toward a bench at the side of the
court. He sounds tired.

"Sorry. I didn't mean to come in so hard. You okay?"

"I'm fine."

"I have some Gatorade in the car if you're thirsty."

He grins. "You're never going to let me live that down, are you?"

"Dude. Gatorade is scientifically formulated to provide maximum electrolytes. How could you expect coconut water to beat it?"

"I didn't say I expected coconut water to beat it; I said I wanted it to. It's called rooting for the underdog—a concept someone with your competitive streak might not understand."

"Pssh." I shake my head. "Remind me to bet against you on the March Madness brackets."

Chris is still rubbing his side, but I know I didn't hurt him that bad. Something else is bothering him. I wait for him to tell me, but he says nothing. Finally, to break the silence, I ask the question that's been burning a hole in my mind for the past sixteen hours. I know I shouldn't bring it up, but I can't help it. I try to sound casual. "So, what did you and Lindsay end up doing last night?"

Chris buries his face in the towel and makes a show of wiping his forehead. "Fight, mostly."

"Oh?" Trouble in paradise? My heart kicks up a happy dance inside my chest. Stupid heart. "What about?"

He shakes his head. "Nothing. She's a tad annoyed with me right now. We'll work it out." He leans back on the bench and stares at the sky. "I asked her to prom." Something about the way he says it seems almost like a confession, as though he doesn't want to tell me. My heart stops dancing and starts pounding. Can he sense my jealousy? Is that why things have become so awkward between us?

I hold up my hand and give him a high five. "That's awesome." I hope the enthusiasm in my voice doesn't sound too forced. "Gosh, that's kind of a long ways away." Seven weeks. And seven hours, not that I'm counting. He must really be into her if he's looking that far ahead. Or maybe he felt like he had to ask her to make up for the fighting?

Chris's eyes meet mine. "I need to ask you something. You don't have to answer if you don't want."

I nod and brace myself. Does he want my advice on dealing with a pissed off girlfriend? Or—ugh—maybe my opinion on whether he should make a move now that they've been dating for almost two weeks? Or—double ugh—is he going to ask about my own spectacularly lame love life?

He leans forward and rests his elbows on his knees. "Remember that time in the seventh grade when a bunch of us decided to play dodgeball behind the school?"

Um. Okay. That would've been my next guess. I shrug. "I don't know. Maybe?"

"You were captain, and out of all the kids at Sterling Middle, you picked me first to be on your team."

"Okay."

"Why?"

"Why what?"

"Why me? I was a total doofus back then. There were at least ten other guys, and a bunch of girls, who would have been better picks."

What the ... ? "Probably because you were my best friend, and I wanted you on my team?"

"Yeah, well. It didn't work out too great for you. Jacob

Blackwell knocked me out in the first round. Pounded me right here." He points to his left shoulder.

"Wow. Good memory." Who knew dodgeball scars ran so deep? "So you're bringing this up now because … ?"

Chris looks away and begins tapping his left foot. "It just seemed like a strange move; that's all. I mean, you're so intent on winning all the time, and—"

"Chris! It was dodgeball, not the Olympics."

"I think you felt sorry for me. It was a pity pick." His voice takes on an edge. He's upset, and I have no idea why. Maybe I did jab him too hard.

"Listen. I'm not sure what's going on with you. I'm sorry I elbowed you. And I guess I'm sorry I picked you first in dodgeball, though that seems like an odd thing to hold a grudge about after all this—"

"It's not a grudge. That's not the point. Don't you see?" Chris lets out a frustrated groan and again shifts his gaze toward the sky.

"No. I don't see." I grab his chin and turn it toward me. "Explain."

He blinks and reaches up to grab my hand. "It's …" His voice trails off, and for a moment, sitting so close, I feel as though I'm swallowed up in his blue eyes. The sadness that lurks there disorients me. His hand slides down my wrist and up my arm. His touch is so light, so tentative. I lean toward him, silently willing him to keep going, to run his hands over my shoulders, up to my neck, to draw me close, and—

His cell phone rings, and he pulls away, snapping me back to reality. He checks the screen and sighs. "Sorry."

"Is that Lindsay?"

"Yeah."

"You should take it." I choke the words out. What's wrong with me? Chris has a girlfriend. One he has asked to prom. A girl I set him up with, for crying out loud. I need to wake up and deal with it.

Chris wanders across the court. I can't hear what he's saying, but his tone of voice is uncharacteristically sharp. They're obviously still arguing.

Chris slips his phone into his pocket and trudges back toward me. "I gotta go."

"Everything okay?"

"She's having issues with her mom right now. I feel like she needs someone to talk to."

I nod and wave him toward his car. "Go. Definitely. You're a good boyfriend." It's true. I only wish I weren't so petty as to hold that against him.

He pauses as he opens his car door. "I'm really sorry, Lex. Rain check?"

I give him a thumbs-up. "Sounds good." This morning isn't turning out the way I'd planned anyway. Why can't Chris just tell me what's bothering him? We've been best friends for eight years—or at least I thought we have. Who knew he resented being picked first in dodgeball? What other transgressions has he been holding against me all this time?

I grab the ball and challenge myself to a game of half court hero. Spin to the left, spin to the right, up and … *swish*! Holy cannoli. I turn to see if Chris is watching, but he's already pulled away. I spend the next half hour trying to repeat the shot and wondering whether something can legitimately be called a rain check when there's not a cloud in the sky.

Chapter
TWENTY-EIGHT

The next week is completely crazy. I have so many Boyfriend Whisperer assignments, I barely have time to think about Chris and Lindsay. That is, until Thursday afternoon when Lindsay shouts to me as I'm rounding the corner to F Hall on my way to meet Abi.

"Lexi, there you are!"

I twirl around. What's she doing here? No one ever comes down to this part of the school. "Hey, Lindsay. 'Sup?"

"Chris and I have missed you at lunch this week. Where've you been?"

I shrug. I doubt they've missed me at all, though I suppose it's sweet of her to say so. "Lots of projects due."

"Oh, I know. Isn't it ridiculous? It's like the teachers don't realize we have lives." Lindsay leans in a little. "Anyway, I wanted to ask if you'd like to come bowling with us Saturday morning. We're going to check out that new place in Leesburg."

Bowling? She doesn't strike me as the type. No pun intended. "Um. Like I said, I'm pretty swamped right now with all my—"

"Oh, come on." She gives my arm a playful slap. "It'll be fun. Take a couple hours off to hang with your friends."

Friends. Is that what we are? Because I can barely handle being around her. I take a deep breath. She's right, of course. And I'm being petty, as usual. And if I want to stay friends with Chris—and let's face it, no stupid crush is worth losing my best friend over, even if they do happen to be the same person—maybe I need to start making Lindsay my friend, too. "Sure," I say, again forcing a smile. "You're absolutely right. A couple of hours can't hurt."

I circle around and down another hallway until I'm sure she's gone before heading back toward the closet. The late bell is going to ring in about two minutes, and Abi's going to kill me.

Sure enough, she's standing just inside the door, tapping her foot. "Do you even care that I'm going to be late to P.E.? One more after this and Mr. Hawk will give me detention."

"Sorry, but Lindsay cornered me on my way over here. She wants me to go bowling with her and Chris Saturday." I shudder.

"Bowling? What's that about?"

"I have no idea. It's not important. Why did you need to see me?"

"You'd better be careful with that girl, Lexi. She's a total wench. I don't trust her."

I give Abi a weak smile. If I weren't her boss, and if we weren't so different, she'd be a great person to have as a friend. "It's just bowling. And actually, Lindsay has been nothing but nice to me. I can't point to a single reason to hate her. Other than the obvious. If anything, I'm the one who's been the wench."

"Oh, please. 'Nice' is not in Lindsay's wheelhouse. She's playing you. If there were such a thing as frequent liar miles, that girl would have been to Saturn and back." Abi swipes at her phone and checks the time. "Dammit. I really need to go. I just wanted to warn you that I've been hearing some rumblings."

"Rumblings?"

"Yeah. Apparently a whole group of girls from the volleyball team are pissed at you … at the Boyfriend Whisperer. Something about Jenna Matthews dating one of their brothers and then totally cheating on him."

"What? I'm supposed to police my clients? And anyway, who the heck is Jenna Matthews? She wasn't *even* a client."

"Doesn't matter. They think she was. They're on a mission to out you."

"Well, tell them she wasn't our client. Tell them I've never heard of her."

Abi tilts her head. "Like they'll believe me. They know I'd never betray the client-whisperer privilege." The bell rings, and she squeezes her eyes shut. "Great. The things I do for this stupid job."

I give her a quick hug. "You're the best, Abi. And don't worry about the rumblings. It'll blow over."

Boy's got form. I can't help but admire it as Chris sends the ball sailing down the alley for his fourth strike of the morning. Unbelievable. The last time we bowled was about two years ago, and he was lucky to get a spare or two. Now he's hefting around a sixteen-pound ball and knocking down the pins like a pro.

The Leesburg alley is brand new—one of those super-fancy spots with glow-in-the-dark balls, neon blue light strips lining the gutters, and giant screens playing sports at the other end of the lanes. We're sipping on fancy juice smoothies and munching on pita bread with hummus as we play. Part of me longs for the scuffed-up floorboards and overcooked hot dogs of our old alley. Back in the day, Chris and I spent hours messing around on the lanes and in the arcade room, and I never gave a single thought to his stupid form.

"Have you been secretly practicing?" I ask as we bump fists.

"If you count the Wii. It's all about the follow through." He pulls a super-serious face and demonstrates his arm motion.

Lindsay wraps her arm around Chris's waist. "What can't this guy do?" She beams as she gazes up at him. "I'm a lucky girl, Chris Broder."

Yes. Yes, you are.

She stands on her tiptoes to kiss him, so I turn away and hold my already bone-dry hands over the ball-return hand dryer. *Never mind me. Just a third wheel spinning uselessly over here.*

"You're up, Lexi." Chris scoots toward the lobby. "I'm going to run to the bathroom."

Lindsay and I watch as he lopes off.

"Does he seem different to you this morning?" Lindsay asks.

"What?"

"Does Chris seem any different?"

I shrug. "I don't know. Why?"

Lindsay gives me a sly smile. "It took him forever, but he finally made a move last night."

"Oh?" Half of me wants to run screaming from this conversation, but the other half needs to know exactly what "move" she's referring to. A look-different-the-next-morning move sounds … ugh. On the other hand, I don't think I want to know.

"He was amazing. Truly." Lindsay's eyes are practically the size of the bowling balls, and her conspiratorial smile leaves little doubt as to what she's talking about.

"Wow … that's …" I try to sound casual, to hide the funhouse of images and emotions tumbling around inside me. *Breathe, Lexi.*

Lindsay lays her hand on my arm. "Are you okay?"

"Yeah. Fine."

She gives me a hug. "I'm so glad we're friends."

I grab a ball and turn away. I do not want to be this girl's friend, cannot be her friend, if it means she plans to confide in me about girl things. Not when she's dating Chris. No way. No, sir. No, thank you.

I must have picked up Chris's ball, because when I sling my arm back, it feels like—well, like a really heavy bowling ball—and I barely succeed in bringing it forward. It slams onto the floor and crashes straight into the gutter. Awesome. Tears spring to my eyes, so I watch the ball make its excruciatingly slow trip to the end of the lane and into the abyss as I try to blink them away.

"You might want to go back to the eleven pounder." Chris has come up behind us.

I swivel around. "You think?" It comes out as a bit of a shriek.

"Whoa. Just a suggestion." He eyes me warily. "You okay?"

I grit my teeth. "Actually, no. I don't feel well." I'm not angry, really. More … shaken. Chris apparently has done something with a girl that I've never even come close to doing with a guy. My Chris. My best friend, who wouldn't even try the high dive at the pool or the Intimidator Coaster at King's Dominion without me beside him, encouraging him. Not that I would have wanted to be beside him last night, obviously, but … crap. "I think I'm going to head out."

Chris walks toward me, concern in his eyes. "You do seem a little pale. You all right to drive? Because I could drive you home in your car and Lindsay can follow in mine."

Lindsay appears at his side. "That's nice of you, Chris, but I can't drive a stick."

"Apparently, you can." I blurt this without thinking.

Lindsay bursts into giggles, and Chris glances back and forth between us. "What?"

"Nothing. Listen, I'll be fine. You guys finish my game." I force a smile, but on the way out, I stop in the ladies' room. The hummus wasn't that great going down, but it's positively disgusting coming back up.

Chapter
TWENTY-NINE

For the next week, I avoid Chris and Lindsay as much as possible. I fake a headache and spend Tuesday afternoon in the nurse's office to get out of chem lab. I can't deal. I really can't. But Friday is an A Day, and I know I have to face them eventually, so I force myself to walk into the cafeteria and sit at their table.

Dammit. When did I start thinking of it as *their* table?

"There she is." Chris's smile is almost enough to lift my sour mood.

"Where do you stand on matching ties?" Lindsay accosts me before I can even set down my tray.

Chris widens his eyes and shakes his head, and she slaps his chest. "No signaling."

I look from one to the other. "Matching ties? What kinds of ties, and what are they supposed to match?"

Massey groans. Apparently, he's had enough of whatever conversation I've walked into.

"Sorry, sorry." Lindsay laughs and waves her hands around in an apology. "We were having a discussion about prom. I bought a red dress. Should Chris or should Chris not wear a matching red tie?"

"Um. I don't know. I guess I've never really given ties much thought." I want to ask, *what difference does it make since the two of you will no doubt tear off your stupid red dress and your tux and make mad, passionate love halfway through the night anyway?* But I refrain. Instead, I mumble, "He should wear whatever looks best on him, I suppose."

Lindsay pouts. "You're no fun." She leans across the table and lowers her voice. "So, who are you going to prom with?"

Massey snorts, and I shoot him a dirty look. Is it so unthinkable that I would go to prom with someone? I shrug and bite into my slice of pepperoni pizza. "I dunno."

"Okay. Let me ask it this way: Who do you *want* to go with? Who do you like?"

My face grows warm. Despite the fact that I am very specifically *not* looking at Chris, I can feel him staring at me. My throat closes up, and I have to force the pizza down. I roll my eyes and try to assume a casual tone. "This is why I tend to hang out with guys instead of girls. Not a single boy has ever asked me that question." I smile coyly. "Maybe there's someone. Maybe not."

Massey slams down his empty soda can, crushing it against his tray. "Enough about prom. Let's talk about after prom. Party at Briggsy's. It's going to be massive. He's getting a band and everything."

Hmm. Much as I'd like to continue to steer away from the topic of prom rather than back toward it, I can't help but ask. "Who's Briggs going with?"

Massey shakes his head. "As of right now, no one. He's still hung up on that little snot, Abi."

"What? Abi's not a snot. She's a sweetheart. Briggsy's the one who—" Oops. All three of them are staring at me.

"Since when are you and Abi so tight?" Massey asks.

"We're not. I just … when she and Briggsy were together, we hung out sometimes. She's nice. And you have to admit he can be kind of a jerk, what with all of his extracurricular flirting."

Massey shakes his head. "That's the problem with you girls. If a guy pays too much attention, you complain he's smothering you, but if he so much as looks at another girl, you call him a jerk. We can't win."

"Oh, please." Lindsay points a celery stick at him. "We're not that complicated. Guys simply don't make an effort to figure out what we want." She grins up at Chris. "Except for you. You're perfect." She gives him a quick kiss. "And feel free to smother me, by the way. I'm all about being smothered with attention."

I toss my pizza crust onto my tray. This was a mistake. The two of them are like nails on a chalkboard. Every time they touch I want to scream. And the thought of them together—*together* together—turns my stomach. I need to get out of here. I pull out my phone and pretend to check my texts. I hold it up and nod vaguely toward the door. "Coach Reilly needs to see me. I should—"

"It's Jerod, isn't it?" Chris's eyes bore through me. He's

sitting with his arms crossed in front of his chest, his back slumped casually against his chair, but I can hear the tap, tap, tap of his left foot beneath the table.

"What?" I gesture again toward my phone. "I just told you. It's Coach Reilly."

"Not that." He leans forward and rests his arms on the table, his expression serious. "You said you liked someone. Jerod."

"I said *maybe* I liked someone, and …" I tug at my ponytail, flustered. "And it's really none of your business who that is."

"It's my business if it's Jerod."

"What? Why? Why would you possibly care if I liked Jerod?"

Chris glances away. "I don't want you to get hurt; that's all."

Too late for that.

"How exactly would I get hurt by liking Jerod? Speaking theoretically, of course."

Chris's lips twitch, and he still won't meet my eyes. "Just be careful."

There's something he's not telling me. Half of me is dying to know what that is, but the other half decides I'm being silly because I do not, in fact, like Jerod. As I push back my chair and grab my books, Lindsay leans over and gives Chris another kiss. And another. I clench my teeth.

Wonder how Jerod feels about matching ties? Speaking theoretically, of course.

Chapter
THIRTY

I fake to the left and dribble to the right, around my opponent, unobstructed to the basket. It's a gorgeous layup, off the board and through the hoop. For zero points. *Come on, Lexi! We need points!*

"Come on, Lexi." Mom reaches back from the front seat of the Land Cruiser and shakes my leg. "We're here. We're at the campus. You okay?"

I gasp and clutch at my seatbelt, struggling to breathe. "I'm fine," I say finally. "Bad dream. Annoying dream."

This is my first college visit—to Virginia Tech, in the middle of nowhere in the heart of the Blue Ridge Mountains. Why in the world would anyone put a university out here? I'm filled with a vague sense of dread as we rumble past a huge "Home of the Hokies" sign outside the football stadium and pull into a spot by a massive indoor arena.

What the heck is a Hokie, anyway?

Dad grins at me in the rearview mirror. "Ready for this?"

I shrug. Ready as I'll ever be, I suppose.

"Now, now. How about some enthusiasm?" Mom is smiling, but her tone is sharp. "Tech has made you a very generous offer. I expect you to show some gratitude."

I nod and force a smile. She's right, of course. Tech is an awesome school, and lots of kids would kill to be in my place. But knowing I'm acting like an ungrateful brat doesn't make me feel any better. It also doesn't make me feel any more grateful or any less bratty. I don't want to be here, staring down a path to four more years of scorecards and stat sheets. The tightness in my chest intensifies.

The assistant coach who greets us is sweet, bordering on perky. "Laurel Jackson. You can call me Laurel." My dad doffs his Wizards cap at her. In case she missed it.

Laurel leads us straight into the arena, and my heart skips a beat in spite of myself. It's enormous. Two guys are jumping rope at the far end, and the tappity-tap of their feet and the hard plastic ropes echo through the cavernous space.

"This is where all the magic happens." Laurel makes a wide, sweeping motion. "Cassell Coliseum seats a little over ten thousand people—not that the women's games fill it up, but ..." she gives me a hopeful smile. "If we can win a championship or two, we could probably come close."

A door slams behind us and three girls walk in.

"Ah, look who it is." Laurel ratchets up from cheerful to positively beaming. "Here's someone you might remember."

One of the girls does seem familiar, and as she comes closer, I recognize her. Of course, Madeleine. I forgot she came here. We played together at Grand View. We rarely spoke off the court, because (a) she was a senior, and even though I was a varsity starter, I was still a lowly freshman, and (b) she was a heck of a lot more popular than me, always talking about parties and guys and crazy weekends at the beach and stuff I know almost nothing about even to this day.

Why do adults assume that kids who went to school together are all friends? Don't they remember what it was really like? Based on my *Veronica Mars* binge watching, I'm thinking things haven't changed that much since Lauren was my age. Does graduating somehow wipe clean those memories?

"Hey, Lexi. Good to see you." Madeleine gives me a quick hug. "This is Jolene Renner and LaMaurianna Watson."

"Everyone calls me Mo," LaMaurianna says. She glances at Lauren, who gives her a nod. "We have something for you." She pulls out from behind her back a Tech t-shirt. It's orange and maroon and has my name on the back with the number eleven—the same as my high school number.

"Oh my gosh, that's so nice." I take it and hold it up for size. "I can't believe you did this. You shouldn't have."

They really shouldn't have. I don't deserve this. This whole visit is basically me barreling down a track to nowhere because I don't know how to stop the train.

All three girls—even Madeleine—give me genuine smiles that make me feel even worse. "Hope to see you here next year," Jolene says.

"We gotta run, but Coach will give you my email address if you need anything," Madeleine says. She gives me another hug before they take off.

Lauren grins. "Ready for the tour?" She takes us around and shows us the Coliseum and then leads us to a whole other building they use just for practice. She takes us through the workout rooms, the locker rooms, and a classroom set up to watch film. My mom's eyes shine, and I know exactly what she's thinking. Watching video of my every shot would be so much more thorough than simply recording them on stat sheets. Yay.

Finally, we wind up outside the head coach's office, and Lauren checks her Fitbit. "We're a few minutes early to meet with Coach. Can I get you anything? Do you have any questions?"

"What's a Hokie?"

"Lexi." My mom shakes her head.

"It's a legit question."

Lauren laughs. "The name comes from an old fight song. But Hokie is actually a type of stone. You'll see it in a lot of the buildings on campus."

"A stone?" I raise my eyebrows and nod. "Interesting." It's not. It's the most boring thing in the history of things.

A door behind Lauren opens and Coach steps into the room. I've seen him on TV, but he looks even bigger in person. "Alexis?" He shakes my hand.

"Lexi."

"Of course." He offers a sweeping wave, urging my parents and me into the room. "Let's chat."

Coach gets right to the point, explaining what he wants to accomplish with his team for the next few years and how he plans to get there. "I know you play forward now, but we'd need you as a point guard."

"Oh?" My stomach does a little twirl. "Interesting." This time, I mean it, though I kind of wish I didn't. Changing to point guard would be a challenge, and I have to admit I rather like the idea of directing the offense. *If* I decide to play.

Coach leans forward. "Lexi, you've received our scholarship offer. I don't expect you to make a decision on the spot, but if you commit within the next sixty days, that scholarship will be guaranteed for your four years here at Virginia Tech, even if, God forbid, you injure yourself during your senior year of high school and can't play a single game."

"Wow. Thank you."

"That's wonderful," my mom says, and Dad nods in agreement.

"What if I suck?"

"Excuse me?" Coach appears startled. "I don't believe I—"

I feel my mom's eyes shooting darts, but I can't help myself. "What if I stay healthy, but I suddenly start to suck? Say I lose my touch and my three-point percentage drops way down—what then? Or what if I decide to quit basketball altogether?"

"Well ..." Coach shuffles a small stack of papers on his desk and shifts in his chair. "The scholarship is contingent on you playing as long as you're healthy, but I can't imagine with your demonstrated skill sets that you'd—"

"I apologize, Coach." Mom lays her hand on my arm and presses down hard. "Lexi's a bit nervous about all of this. It's a big step. And she's prone to thinking about worst-case scenarios."

I want to point out that neither losing my touch at basketball nor deciding to hang up my high-tops would be the worst-case scenario. Did she not hear Coach just pose the possibility of a career-ending injury? Surely that would be worse. But the look in her eyes tells me not to go there, so I bite back my words, take the deepest breath I can given the fact that my chest once again feels as though a sumo wrestler has plopped down on top of it, and offer what I hope passes for an apologetic smile.

Chapter
THIRTY-ONE

Chris slides onto the stool next to me and tosses his chemistry book on the table. "Congrats."

"Thanks, but it's not over yet." I'm in first place in our March Madness pool, but there are still a few games to go, and Briggsy is right behind me.

"It is for me. I should never have picked North Carolina. They didn't have a chance."

"Yes, well." I give him my sorry-not-sorry look. "I tell you every year to take emotion out of it. Sentimentality is for losers. You're supposed to pick who you think will win, not who you *wish* would win." I cough into my hand. "Coconut water."

Chris laughs and punches my arm. It's a light punch, not intended to hurt, but I recoil from it. Knowing what he and Lindsay have been up to makes physical contact with him unbearable. Is he in love with her? I mean, obviously he really, really likes her if they're doing *that*, but does he love her? Part of me doesn't want to know, but part of me needs to find out.

Just before the bell rings, Lindsay rushes in. She pauses and gives Chris a kiss on the cheek before flitting off to her lab table.

I lean in and whisper. "So, you two are getting pretty serious, huh?"

Chris shrugs. "I don't know."

"Oh, come on. You're practically attached at the hip. And I see the way she looks at you."

"Yeah, I guess."

I sigh. "Chris, I'm your best friend." It kills me to say it, but I force myself. "If you're falling in love with her, you can tell me. That's the kind of thing friends tell each other."

His face registers somewhere between confusion and amusement. "Falling in love? Now who's being sentimental?" He shakes his head. "She's a great girl, and I like her and all, but ... love? Huh uh."

Ms. Gupta appears at our table. "Chris? Lexi? I apologize for interrupting your very important conversation, but in case you've failed to notice, I am trying to call the class to order. Perhaps there is something you would like to share?"

Giggles erupt from behind us, and I bite at the inside of my lip. Chris shakes his head, sending Ms. Gupta away.

This was, in fact, a very important conversation—important and disturbing. Could he really mean what he just said? *A great girl.* Seriously?

"Actually, I do have something I'd like to share." I stand, ignoring the alarm in Chris's eyes.

Ms. Gupta regards me warily. "Yes?"

"It's … it's something I noticed last night. My dad was making shepherd's pie for dinner, and I was helping him. You know, peeling the potatoes and mashing them."

Everyone is staring at me as though I'm crazy. Which clearly I am. Ms. Gupta nods. "I see. And what did you notice?"

"Well, he put it in the oven to bake, and it was supposed to take forty minutes, but I was starving, so I jacked up the temperature, figuring it would cook faster. Only it didn't. It just burnt the top. The meat was practically raw."

Jason Marks snickers and puts on his best Soup Nazi accent. "No shepherd's pie for you!"

"Exactly." I point at him. "And my dad was really ticked off."

Jason rolls his eyes. "What's your point, Malloy?"

"The point is, sometimes if you rush things, you can do more harm than good. The potatoes couldn't handle all that heat, and they paid the price. It would have been better to go slow so the insides could catch up with the outside. I mean … if the inside isn't ready, you need to let it cook longer until it is. Don't go cranking up the heat."

Ms. Gupta knits her eyebrows together. "Are we still talking about food?"

"Um. Yes." I sit back down and glance at Chris, who appears completely mystified. "This was a true story. True and tragic. And a waste of a perfectly good shepherd's pie."

"I see." Ms. Gupta points her stylus at me. "So tell me, Lexi. Why did the potatoes burn while the meat did not cook?"

"It's like I said. I turned the temperature too high."

"Yes? And?"

I glance around, hoping for some help from my classmates, but I'm the one who started this thing, and they seem to have no interest in bailing me out. "Because … heat … and … chemistry?"

Ms. Gupta sighs and launches into a lecture about moisture and dryness and something called the Maillard reaction while I concentrate on breathing and not throttling Chris's neck. When class ends, I grab my stuff and dart toward the door.

"Hey." Chris follows right behind. "Lexi, hold up."

I don't want to talk to him. I don't even want to see him. One minute he tells me he's not "like that" and the next, he's messing around with a "great girl." So which is it?

"Lexi." He grabs my arm. "What was that about?"

"What?"

"The taking it slow and the heat and the burnt potatoes. What were you talking about?"

I shrug. "You heard Ms. Gupta. It's the Maillard reaction. Who knew?"

"Come on. You and I both know you weren't talking about shepherd's pie. That was about Jerod, wasn't it?"

Jerod? What the— "What are you talking about?"

"Have you been seeing him? Has he tried something?"

"What? No. What? Why would you—"

Chris pulls me to the side of the hallway and lowers his voice. "I asked around about him after the Virginia Beach tournament. Dude's a player. You should stay away from him."

I blink. My mind doesn't know what to do with this information. Chris looked into Jerod? So maybe the flirting did bother him, and he wants to protect me—like a sister, no doubt, but still, it's awfully sweet. On the other hand, who is he to talk? He can mess around with Lindsay, but I have to avoid Jerod?

I shrug out of his grip and turn to leave. "Appreciate the warning, but I'm a big girl. It's under control, thank you very much."

Chapter
THIRTY-TWO

I stare at the phone. My heart rate is out of control. I've never called a boy before. Well, actually, I've called lots of boys—Chris, Briggs, Massey. But not like this. Not to ask a guy on a date. What do I say? What if he says no? Or, what if it goes to voicemail? What then?

Come on, Lexi. You can do this. You're the Boyfriend Whisperer for crying out loud.

I pace my bedroom and remind myself that I don't actually even like Jerod. I mean, he's nice enough. And cute. And it's possible that I *could* like him after a date or two. He's just … not Chris. But Chris doesn't like me. He's with Lindsay. As in, *with* her.

Is that why I'm doing this? To get back at Chris? I don't let myself think about that. Instead, I take a deep breath and dial Jerod's number. I think a million thoughts as the phone rings. What if he wasn't flirting in Virginia Beach? He probably wasn't. I mean, there were a dozen cheerleaders there, all prettier than me. I must have looked like a big, awkward idiot next to all of them. Just because he smiled at me and complimented my hair, all of a sudden I think he's in love with me? Maybe he was merely trying to make one of those cheerleaders jeal—

"Hello?"

Ack! Why couldn't it have gone to voicemail?

"Jerod? Hey." My voice comes out as a squeak, so I clear my throat. "This is Lexi. Lexi Malloy."

"Well, hello, Lexi Malloy."

"How's it going?"

"Good. Awesome. Especially now. To what do I owe this pleasure?"

I take a deep breath. So far, so good. He hasn't hung up on me. I haven't puked. I'm speaking in complete sentences. Mostly. "Um. Well. I was wondering. So there's this party Saturday night." My voice shakes. My whole body shakes. Man, I don't give my clients enough credit for putting themselves out there. Coming up with a plan for whispering a boy is the easy part. Actually carrying it out is torturous.

"Lexi? You still there?"

"Yes, sorry."

"You were saying something about a party? Because there's nothing I like better than a good party. I hope you were about to invite me."

I smile. "Thank you."

"For what?"

"For making that easier."

His voice is deep and warm and smooth. "My pleasure."

Dear Anita:

Thank you for entrusting Boyfriend Whisper Enterprises with your matchmaking needs. If you follow my instructions precisely, you are guaranteed to secure a date with Jose Ramos within three weeks or your money back. Your first set of instructions is as follows:

I read over my standard introduction. Ugh. It's all wrong. This poor girl is about to embark on a terrifying journey, and I'm using words like "precisely" and "secure"? Sounds like a legal document rather than a plan for finding love. I hit delete and start over.

Dear Anita:

Thank you for contacting Boyfriend Whisper Enterprises in your search for amor!

Amor. Is that too much? Anita's first language is Spanish, but maybe that's going overboard. Hmm. What if it is? So sue me. I flex my hands and continue.

If you follow these instructions, you are guaranteed to win Jose Ramos's heart.*

First, let me congratulate you. You've taken a big step by contacting me. But it is only the first step. You have some hard work ahead of you. You will need to be fearless and persistent, but as they say, nothing in life worth having comes easily. You've got this!

Here's what I need you to do:
First, rent the 1972 movie *The Candidate* starring Robert Redford. This is one of Jose's favorite movies. Watch it and take notes on the debate portion. (It's actually a pretty good movie if you can get past the hairstyles!)

Second, show up at the end of Jose's Debate Team practice on Wednesday with brownies. He loves peanut butter best, but one of the girls on the team is allergic, so you'd better make them plain chocolate, with no nuts. Remember, these are NOT for Jose, they're simply a treat for the whole team. No need to be shy—everyone loves brownies!

Finally, ask someone on the team—anyone, girl or boy, so long as you ask loud enough for Jose to hear—if they've ever seen *The Candidate*. Mention that it has a great debate scene in it and say that you really enjoy watching good debates. Jose will undoubtedly come talk to you about the movie since you'll probably be the first person he's ever met who's seen it. Share some of your favorite quotes from the debate. Smile and be friendly, but no serious flirting yet. And no further contact until my next email.

Good luck! And remember, with Boyfriend Whisperer Enterprises, "Love is but a whisper away."

Sincerely,
The Boyfriend Whisperer
www.boyfriendwhispererenterprises.com

* Guaranteed within three weeks or your money back.

As I scan the email, my fingers itch to go back in and delete some of the sap. Maybe Chris is right. Maybe I am getting sentimental. I resist the urge and hit "send." I've done my part. Now it's up to Anita to make it happen.

Chapter
THIRTY-THREE

I take a sip of soda and check my phone for the millionth time. Where's Jerod? He had to work this afternoon, so he offered to meet me at the party. He'd better get here soon. I am literally standing in a corner next to a potted plant trying to be inconspicuous, which is tough when you're as tall as me and the only girl in the room who apparently missed the memo on the mini skirts.

The fact that I'm crashing uninvited doesn't help. I figured bringing a hot guy from another school would make up for it. What if he doesn't show?

Abi shoots me a sweet and slightly apologetic smile from across the room. I know she'd come talk to me if she could, but of course, she can't. People might notice, and then they might wonder, and then they might start to surmise. The last thing I need is a bunch of surmising classmates. I nod in her general direction and plaster on a smile. The second-to last thing I need is Abi feeling sorry for me.

The front door opens, and my heart pauses. As anxious as I am for Jerod to arrive, part of me is terrified for that moment when he walks in and sees me standing here, friendless in my jeans and a hoodie. "Hey, dude." I hear the voice before I see him. It's not Jerod, it's Chris, followed closely by Lindsay. Crap.

I knew they'd be here, of course. If I'm being honest, that's partly the point. A round of backslapping and fist bumping and hugging and squealing ensues. Chris flows through the room as easily as a fish through water, and it occurs to me that he and Lindsay are officially a Grand View power couple. He somehow has moved into the middle of this crowd, this life, as though it's where he's always belonged, while I stand on the edge with the plant life.

I catch my breath as he turns and spots me. Though I am by far the most fully clothed girl in the room, I feel naked, exposed. He tilts his head and squints as though he's trying to place me—like when you're at the beach, and you see someone from back home, and your brain requires an extra beat to process it.

"Hey, Lexi." He walks over. The lighting is dim, but I could swear he's blushing. "What are you doing here? I mean, it's cool that you're here. I just didn't expect to see you. And what's that?" He frowns into my cup.

"Sprite," I mumble. I don't need to further stand out as the only girl in the room not drinking beers and wine coolers.

"Good. Stick with Sprite."

His approving nod annoys me, so I decide to give him something to disapprove of. "I'm meeting Jerod. He should be here any minute."

"Jerod? So you two are …?"

I shrug. "Whatever. It's just a party." As though meeting up with boys at random parties is simply how I roll.

"Lexi!" Lindsay rushes over. "What a nice surprise. I didn't realize you were friends with Elana."

I offer a careless wave of my hand. "Yeah, we go way back." I'm pretty sure she knows I'm lying.

She gives me an awkward hug and a once over. "You look … cute." I force a smile. I suppose one good lie deserves another. She screeches and rushes off at the sight of an as-yet-unhugged friend across the room, and I turn to Chris.

"I'm not sure I even know which one is Elana."

He laughs and motions to a girl standing in the stairwell talking on her phone. "Over there. Elana Medford."

"Okay. She's familiar." I'm pretty sure she's on the swim team, though of course she looks different fully clothed. Or, well, half-clothed.

"So this is how the 'in-crowd' does Saturday nights, huh?"

Chris shrugs. "I guess. They like their parties."

They? So he doesn't even realize yet that he's one of them—that he swept in here as naturally as his finger-roll layup.

A couple stumbles past us, clearly wasted. The guy is waving his arms in the air, ranting—something about a screwed up tattoo and the cost of getting it removed.

"And what about you? Do you like their parties?"

Another shrug. "Better than sitting at home playing video games, I guess."

Ouch. I know that wasn't aimed at me, but it still stings. Can I help it if I like to take out my frustrations blasting piggies? Anyway, I'd rather hang out with Stella, Matilda, and Red than with Unfortunate Tattoo Guy any day.

As if he's read my mind, Chris leans toward me, his voice low. "There are a few idiots, but most of these guys are pretty cool. And girls. You'll see."

Somehow I don't think I will see, because I can't image hanging out with the mini-skirt crowd on a regular basis. Chris may be comfortable playing center court at a party like this, but I'm more of a back-of-the-bleachers type. "In case you haven't noticed, my only friend until you arrived was Mr. Ficus here." I extend my hand in an introduction. "Chris, meet the ficus tree. Ficus, this is Chris."

He rolls his eyes. "You're whack. Briggs and Massey are here somewhere. And lots of people you know. Sometimes I think you choose to be …" He pauses, searching for the right word.

"Awkward?"

"No. You're not awkward. More like … detached."

"Aloof."

"Aloof! That's it. You need to lose the loof."

"Be more like Lindsay, I guess." I hate myself for saying it, and I hate myself even more for the fact that it comes out kind of whiney.

"What? No way. I mean, she's definitely not aloof."

Chris grins and shakes his head as we watch her hug yet another cheerleader who has walked into the party. "But that's her. You should do you. Just less aloofly."

"I'm going to need you to stop saying that word."

"Aloof?"

"Yes, stop. It's starting to sound really weird."

"A-loooof." He howls it. "You're the one who brought it up."

"I know. I regret it. We should have gone with 'detached.'"

"Oh, come on. Admit it. You *loof* the way I say 'aloof.' Aloof, aloof, aloof."

"Stop." I reach up and clamp my hand over his mouth, but I can't help but giggle. He grabs me in a bear hug and continues mumbling the word "aloof" into my hand over and over. I squirm to get away, but I'm laughing so hard I can't break his hold.

"Hey, there." A voice as smooth as Häagen-Dazs interrupts our scuffle.

"Jerod." Chris releases his grasp.

"Hi. You made it." I step away from Chris, flustered.

"Of course I made it. You invited me." He gives me a broad smile. "Wouldn't miss it." He shakes Chris's hand. "Yo, man. Good to see you."

Chris scowls and draws himself up to his full six-foot-three stature. Or is he six-four now? "What's up?"

"Did I interrupt something?"

"No. In fact, Lexi's been waiting for you. Why are you late?"

I jab Chris with an elbow. It's not like him to be rude.

Jerod gives me puppy dog eyes. "Sorry about that. Got caught working a little past my shift."

I shake my head. "No need to apologize." I turn to Chris. "Jerod works at Veg Out."

"Veg Out?" He says. "Well, that explains the onion smell."

"Chris!" I grab Jerod's arm. "Pay no attention to him. He's just jealous because his job involves scraping gum off of seat bottoms." I give Chris a what-the-heck glare as I lead Jerod off toward the kitchen to check out the drinks. We draw a few stares, but now, instead of feeling weird and self-conscious, I'm all smiles. Who would have thought? Lexi Malloy with a boy—a very cute boy with a gorgeous smile and a voice that'll melt a girl's heart. I slip my arm through his. "Thank you for coming out tonight. This'll be fun."

It will. I'm sure it will. Except that as we round the corner into the kitchen, we run smack into Jose Ramos, who happens to be in a lip lock with a girl, who happens not to be Anita Alvarez.

Chapter
THIRTY-FOUR

I have so many questions: Who is this chick? Is this just a one-time thing or are they dating? If so, for how long? And how did my research come up empty?

Of course, I can't ask. In fact, I have to act as though I don't even notice them. Unless …

I tap Jose on the shoulder, and he reluctantly pulls away from his date, or fling, or whatever she is. His expression is dazed. "Hey."

"Hi, Jose." My voice comes out unnaturally perky, and I pull Jerod forward. "This is Jerod Wilkins. He's from Pine Bridge, and he doesn't know many people here, so I thought I'd introduce him around. Jerod, this is Jose. We have … the same lunch period, maybe?" I'm grasping.

Jose looks at me as though I'm a freak, but he holds out his hand to Jerod. "Nice to meet you."

I gesture toward Mystery Girl. "And who is this? Aren't you going to introduce us?"

"Of course." Jose puts his arm around her and pulls her forward, his face breaking into a goofy smile. "This is Maria. She just moved here from El Salvador. We're from the same town, and we were friends when we were little. We haven't seen each other in almost eight years." He leans forward and whispers loudly, "She always did have a crush on me."

"Qué?" Maria gives him a sideways glance, so he translates that last sentence for her. She laughs and rolls her eyes at us. "No. Yo soy la que le gusta a él."

"She says it's the other way around."

The glint in Jose's eye tells me she's right, or maybe they both are. Childhood sweethearts, reunited after being separated by eight long years and almost two thousand miles. What a beautiful and wonderful story. Except for the whole I'm-getting-paid-to-break-them-up-again part.

They giggle and go back to kissing. Lovely. What the heck am I supposed to do? Technically, when Anita hired me, Jose didn't have a girlfriend. We have a contract now, and Anita has already completed step one. Who knows what plans she may have made for her future with him? With my success rate, she's probably already bought her prom dress, and the shoes to match. I can't abandon her at this point, can I?

"Are you okay, Lexi? You don't look so good." Jerod takes my soda and refills it. "Want to step outside? It's actually pretty warm out there, for March."

I nod. Maybe some fresh air will help. I need to clear

my mind and forget about whispering. Tonight is about Jerod and me and having fun. Besides, if we go outside, maybe Chris will start to wonder where we went.

Nice, Lexi. I scold myself. I'm being both unfair and ridiculous. Unfair because Jerod doesn't deserve that, and ridiculous because Chris more than likely couldn't care less where I am. He has a whole room full of friends to keep him occupied.

"Actually …" I set my Sprite down and take Jerod's hands in mine. "I think maybe I should go home."

"What?"

"I'm sorry. I know you came all the way out here, but inviting you to this party was a bad idea."

"Um. Okay." Jerod's expression wavers between confused and hurt, and I give myself a mental kick.

"I don't mean because of you. I mean because of the party. It sucks. I mean, it's an okay party, but it sucks as a first date."

"So this is a date?"

My face grows warm. "Maybe."

"Maybe's good enough for me. I'm calling it a date. And since you said 'first date,' I'm going to assume there will be at least one more."

I laugh.

"Will there?"

I don't know what to say, so I pass it off. "Ball's in your court for that one."

"Well, in that case, what are you doing next Satur—"

"Yo, dude. I know you." A stumbling, slurring Briggsy interrupts us. He has two girls fawning over him, but he ignores them and gives Jerod and me each a huge hug. "You're that guy from the restaurant."

"You mean Veg Out?"

"No, that Tex-Mex place in Virginia Beach. You were there."

"Oh, right." Jerod holds out his hand. "Jerod Wilkins."

Briggs ignores his hand and gives him another hug. "Roland Briggs, but you can call me Briggsy. That's what all my friends call me, and if you're a friend of Lexi's, you're a friend of mine." He lets go of Jerod and reaches over to hug me again.

I roll my eyes at Jerod and mouth, *sorry*.

He shrugs and pulls Briggsy off of me. "Hey, man, how about you sit down for a while? Want me to get you some water or something?"

"Nah, I don't need no water. I just need my friends. Lexi, you're my friend, right?" Briggs latches back onto me.

Oh, man. I've never seen him drunk before. Dude can be annoying when he's sober, but this is ridiculous. "Yeah, Briggsy. We're friends."

"Good friends?"

"Yep. Good friends."

"What about Abi? Are you and Abi friends?"

I glance around. The two girls with Briggsy are watching us. "Sure, Briggsy." I roll my eyes at them as if to say, *I'm humoring him. Abi and I are not that close. Really.*

"Why doesn't Abi like me?" He straightens up, his face serious, his words slightly less slurred.

"How do you know she doesn't like you? Maybe she does."

"Nah. She broke up with me. And when I try to talk to her, she blows me off. I gave her a hug just now, and she pushed me away."

I glance at his groupies. Maybe it had something to do with them? Or the fact that he's wasted?

"Briggsy, I don't think you're in a condition to talk about this right now. Let's talk Monday, okay?"

Briggs gives me another hug, and this time practically knocks me over. "You're the best, Lexi. I love you, man. I mean, woman. You know what I mean."

Jerod pulls him off of me again. "We were just about to head out, bro. You going to be okay? Do you have a ride home?"

"Oh, yeah. Massey's here somewhere. He's driving me home." Briggs leans over and whispers something in Jerod's ear, then pulls away. "Don't tell her I told you. It's a secret." Briggsy laughs and stumbles off, and the girls follow in his wake.

Jerod shakes his head. "Dude's a trip."

"What did he say to you? What was the secret?"

"No idea." Jerod puts his arm around my waist and leads me toward the door. "He wasn't making any sense. Sounded like he was saying something about a 'boyfriend whisperer.'"

Chapter
THIRTY-FIVE

"**I**'d like a motion to call this meeting to order."

Abi purses her lips and gives me her best head-tilt. "For real? And if I make the motion, who will second it?"

She has a point. "Fine. Never mind the formalities. Let's jump into the agenda."

It's our first official meeting of the staff of Boyfriend Whisperer Enterprises. I'd never called one before because … well, because texts, phone calls, and hastily arranged consultations in the janitor's closet had always sufficed. This afternoon, though, I've reserved a private study room in the back recesses of the Sterling Community Library. Today we have some important business to discuss.

"Agenda item number one: Security." I peer up at Abi. "Anything to report?"

Abi rolls her eyes. She is *so* not into corporate protocol. Maybe I should have brought doughnuts.

"Actually, yes," she says. "I talked to Ari, and he explained a bunch of stuff I didn't understand, but for the most part, you're safe." Abi's brother majors in computer science at George Mason, with a concentration in hacking, or at least that's the joke he likes to tell.

"For the most part? Please elaborate."

"It's complicated." Abi picks up her agenda and absently waves it around. "The website is totally safe, meaning no one can trace it if you used a private registration, which I assume you did."

"Of course."

"And the email is mostly safe, unless …"

"Unless?"

"It seems if someone really, truly, seriously wanted to track down who owns your Boyfriend Whisperer email account, they could do it."

I lean forward in my seat. "How so?"

"If they got the IP address and then matched it to all the IP addresses of everyone's home email in the school, they could eventually find your match."

"You mean match it up with my Gmail IP address?"

"Right. But to do that, they'd have to know your Gmail address in the first place. Not too many people know it, do they? You hardly ever use it."

I groan. "No one except my entire team. Coach insists on communicating with us through email. Very annoying."

"Ugh. That is annoying. But at least no one on your team has a grudge against you—or rather, against the

Boyfriend Whisperer—do they? They wouldn't have any reason to try to track you down."

"Carmella."

"The one with the purple hair? What have we ever done to her?"

"Nothing, but her sister's on the volleyball team."

"Oh." Abi grimaces. "Well, it seems like a long shot, doesn't it? That anyone would go to all that trouble? I don't think you have to worry."

I'm not so sure, so I make a note in my tablet to scope out Carmella later. "Let's move on. Next on the agenda: Anita Alvarez and her BFTB, Jose Ramos."

Abi says nothing, but her lips form a tight, thin line.

Here we go. I take a deep breath. "Go ahead. Say it."

"Say what?"

"You want out."

Abi's metal chair screeches against the floor as she stands. She paces back and forth from one end of the tiny room to the other. "I knew this was going to happen sooner or later. Love isn't something you can plan, like a cheer or a bulk purchase on Accessories.com, or a … a picnic. Sometimes love just happens." Her eyes mist over. "Or doesn't."

Oh, jeez. Dealing with Briggs at that party the other night couldn't have been easy on her. I sigh and motion for her to sit back down. "Abi, I understand what you're saying, but it's our duty to *make* love happen. That's our guarantee to our clients. It's not always easy, but if it were easy, we'd be out of our jobs."

"So … what? We ignore the fact that Jose already has a girlfriend? Did you meet her? She's adorable."

"She's not a girlfriend. She's a girl who's a friend."

"Who makes out with him."

"Come on. She wasn't even in the picture when Anita submitted her application."

"Because she lived in a whole 'nother country. Now she's here, in the United States, *making out with him!*"

I avoid Abi's glare. Part of me knows she's right. Maria seems very sweet, and for all I know, she and Jose are soul mates, meant to be together for all eternity. On the other hand, what can it hurt to give Anita a chance? She deserves a shot. If Jose is supposed to be with Maria, well, surely their relationship could overcome that bump in the road. What's a little love triangle among soul mates?

"I'm not letting Anita down," I say finally. "The poor girl has already started putting herself out there for him—making brownies, watching old movies, showing up randomly at his Debate Team practice. That couldn't have been easy for her. If you want to walk away from the case, go ahead, but I'm in."

Abi makes a vague harrumphing sound and taps her nails on the table. I let her stew, certain that she's coming around to my way of thinking, but instead, she leans forward, her voice hard and low. "Is this about feeling bad for Anita or is it about your precious business?"

"What the …?" She's never spoken to me like this before. "Maybe it's about both. What's wrong with wanting to run a good business?"

"Nothing, but with you, I'm never sure whether it's about running a good business or winning some sort of imaginary game."

"Game? What game?"

"Oh, come on, Lexi. Everything's a competition with you. I'll bet you could tell me right now, off the top of your head, without doing a single calculation, exactly what the Boyfriend Whisperer's success rate is."

Twenty-three out of twenty-four, or 95.8 percent. I purse my lips and look away.

"See. I knew it. But guess what? Those are just numbers. And behind every one of those numbers are human beings with real lives and real feelings, and for every love connection we make, we also could be breaking someone's heart."

"Like Maria's."

"And?" She gives me a meaningful stare.

I bite my lip. I did the right thing accepting Lindsay's application. I believed that then, and I believe it now, and Abi has no right throwing it in my face. I crumple up the agenda. "Screw you. Meeting adjourned."

Chapter
THIRTY-SIX

Mrs. Massey answers the door with a huge bowl of guacamole dip in her right hand and a giant jar of salsa tucked under her left arm. "Hi, Lexi. The boys are all downstairs. Tacos will be ready in a minute."

I grab the condiments from her and head toward the basement. We watch all the games at Massey's, mainly because his mom's idea of TV snacks is so far superior to anyone else's—tacos, ribs, shrimp, gourmet pizzas—and all homemade. Most years, Chris, Briggs, Massey, and I watch the entire March Madness tournament together, but this year was different. We've all had too much going on, and of course, Lindsay is now in the picture. Tonight, though, is the championship game, so we're together. And much to my relief, Lindsay had to stay home to study for a make-up exam.

"You're late," Massey says as I set the food on the bar. "It's bad luck to be late."

"Wake Forest is up by eight." Briggsy's smile tells me he's already counting his winnings.

"It's the first quarter," I say. "Eight points is nothing. Georgetown's a second-half team."

"Where've you been?" Chris scoots over so I can sit next to him on the couch. "It's not like you to be late to a game. Not when you have money on it."

"I know." I avoid his eyes. "Mom cornered me on my way out the door with a lecture about my trig grade. Anyway, don't worry. I caught most of it on the radio."

The second part is true. The first part, not so much. I'm late because I spent half an hour trying to find something remotely cute to wear. The best I could do was a blue zip-up sweater over black tights. Not my usual look but not exactly revolutionary either. None of them seem to notice. "Nice colors, by the way."

Chris is wearing black and gray—Georgetown colors—a real sacrifice for him since he detests the Hoyas. "I'm rooting for you. Mainly because I can't stand the thought of Briggs gloating for the next twelve months."

"If I win, I plan to gloat."

"Of course. I would expect nothing less. But your gloating won't involve constant texts with pictures of you spending the winnings."

"Not my style," I agree. "In fact, I plan to spend it all in one place—on a jean jacket. Already have one picked out." I say this loud enough so Briggs can hear me. "I want to buy something I can wear over and over as a constant reminder of my superior tournament analysis."

Briggs smirks and throws a pillow at me, but I catch it before it hits my face.

"Testing my superior reflexes?"

He tosses a chip, which does hit me, smack on the nose.

"No fair. My hands were full of pillow."

Chris stands, pulls up his sofa cushion, and slams Briggs with it, which results in an impromptu wrestling match—all arms and legs and sneakers flying through the air—and somehow Massey ends up in the middle of it, as well.

Man, I've missed this so much. Tears spring to my eyes, but fortunately, the guys are too busy pummeling each other to notice. Why couldn't we be like this all the time? Why did everything have to change this year? Stupid pheromones. I wish I could go back to thinking of Chris as a friend and just hanging out without all the drama—even if the drama is only in my head.

"Whoa, whoa. Watch that lamp, boys." Mrs. Massey appears at the bottom of the steps with a tray of steaming tacos. She grins and rolls her eyes at me. "Good times, huh?"

I grin. "Actually, yes."

She sets down the tray and surveys the bar. "Oops. Forgot the sour cream. I'll be right back."

I offer to follow and bring it down for her, mainly because I need to compose myself before the guys finish their battle. If they see even a hint of tears, there's no telling what humiliation they'll rain down on me.

We walk into the kitchen to find Mr. Massey loitering over the stove, stirring a pot of what looks like melted chocolate.

"Jeffrey. That's for the kids. I'm making chocolate-covered almonds."

He gives her a look of innocence. "I was merely stirring it so it wouldn't stick to the bottom."

"Mm-hmm." Mrs. Massey walks over and wipes at his chin. "How'd it get up here?"

He grabs her hand and licks it off her finger and kisses her cheek before she shoos him out of the room.

Mrs. Massey turns, a shy smile playing on her lips. "Never mind him. Where were we? Oh, yes. Sour cream." She sifts through her massive refrigerator, checking expiration dates and tossing random containers in the trash. "I just bought a huge thing of it. Where did it go?"

"Mrs. Massey, can I ask you something?"

"Of course."

"How did you and Mr. Massey meet?"

She turns and peers up at me. "You really want to know?"

I nod. It's not like I go around asking people that all the time, but I'm genuinely curious. The two of them seem so in love. Did they look for each other, or did it just "happen"?

"We met online."

"Back then?" This had to be almost twenty years ago.

"Yep. You might say we were early adopters. In those days, you'd never admit to anyone you met that way, though. We concocted this whole story about how we met in the frozen foods section at Safeway."

"Really? Why?"

"I guess people thought those sites were for losers—

people who couldn't get a date on their own. Of course, nowadays everyone and their grandma uses matchmaking services. Aha!" She pulls a tub of sour cream out from the bottom shelf and holds it up victoriously. "I knew it was in there somewhere."

I take it from her. It must weigh five pounds. "So why him?"

"What?"

"Why did you choose Mr. Massey? How'd you know he was the one?"

She tilts her head, considering this. "I didn't at first. I dated a few other guys. Fell head over heels for one of them, in fact, but he turned out to be a jerk." She motions toward the den, where I can hear Mr. Massey cheering at a basket. Hopefully Georgetown's. "I thank God that didn't work out, or I'd never have ended up with this one."

I nod. "So you think it's a good idea to date around?"

"I guess."

Ha! I knew it. I'm doing Anita, Maria, and Jose a favor. Who knows which of the two girls is the right one for him? And how can he decide if he doesn't have a chance to get to know Anita?

"On the other hand…." Mrs. Massey puts her hand on my arm. "If you find the right boy, Lexi—a boy who treats you well and who brings out the best in you—you should hold onto him."

I shake my head. "Oh, no, Mrs. Massey, I think you have the wrong idea. I wasn't asking for myself. I was asking for a … a friend." I couldn't exactly say "client."

"Of course you were, dear." She winks. "Wish your

friend good luck, and remember, sometimes the right boy is someone who—"

"There you are." Chris appears in the doorway. "You're missing the game. Georgetown just tied it up."

"Well, goodness. Isn't it nice of Chris to come looking for you?" Mrs. Massey gives me a meaningful glance as she turns to stir the pot of chocolate. My face grows warm. Can she tell I'm totally crushing on him?

"Sorry. Did I interrupt something?" Chris looks back and forth between us.

"Not at all. I was just grabbing the sour cream." I hold it up as proof that he has walked in on the most mundane of conversations. "It's low-fat," I say, apropos of nothing.

"Um. Okay." He gives a quick wave to Mrs. Massey and ushers me toward the basement door. "Thanks for everything, Mrs. M. The tacos smell great."

I follow him onto the stairwell, but he stops me halfway down. "Actually, I wanted to talk to you about something."

"Sure." I lean against the railing. "What's up?"

"It's about the other night, at the party."

"Yeah?"

"I was wondering … I mean, it seemed like you and Jerod left early, so …"

He noticed when we left? Despite the throngs of friends and admirers? "So?"

"Did you go somewhere else? Or home? Or did you, I don't know … drive around or whatever?"

"Or whatever?" Is it my imagination, or is Chris trying to figure out whether Jerod and I kissed … or whatever? "Would you care to define that?"

"Lexi, I'm not playing." He takes a step toward me, his face serious. "I'm worried about you. I think this guy could be bad news."

I gently push him away. "I assure you, Jerod has been a total gentleman." It's true. He never made a single move on me all night. If Jerod's a player, he's the lamest player ever. Either that, or maybe he's like Chris. Maybe he doesn't really see me as a girl. I push the thought away, bat my lashes at Chris, and pull my best Vivian Leigh imitation. "I do thank you for the concern, though, kind sir."

Chris appears genuinely relieved. I'd love to imagine it's because he's jealous, but I know better. He's playing the protective best friend. "Whoa. Wait a minute." He leans toward me, a scowl crossing his face. "What's this?" He touches the side of my neck, and my hand flies up to the spot.

Jerod and I never even kissed. No way could I have a hickey, but the suggestion that I might and the brush of Chris's fingertips against my skin set my cheeks on fire. I push him away. "You're crazy."

His eyes sparkle, and he laughs. "Gotcha." He taps at the tip of my nose, but he's too slow for my superior reflexes, and I reach up and grab him. It truly is a reflex, and once I'm holding his hand, I'm not quite sure what to do with it. My brain is shouting, *Let it go! Let it go!* But my body is frozen.

Chris twines our fingers together until it's hard to tell whose hand is doing the holding and whose is being held. When he speaks, his voice is soft and low. "Promise you'll be careful, okay? And you won't do anything you don't want to do. And you'll call me if you ever need backup."

I want to tell him not to worry, but he's so close, and his hand feels so perfect in mine, I can't speak. I open my mouth, but no sound comes out.

He leans toward me, his eyes searching mine for ... what? I know Chris better than anyone else on earth and can read his every expression, but he's never looked at me like this before. My heart races and I tilt my head back slightly, and I swear his eyes focus on my lips. Is he going to kiss me? My legs feel weak, and my head spins. I reach for the railing and ... splat!

"What the—" Chris jumps back. Our feet, and half the stairwell, are covered in sour cream.

"Oh, no. Oh my God. Omigod, omigod, omigod." In an instant, Massey and Briggs are at the bottom of the steps, and Mrs. Massey is at the top. They're all staring at me and the great white mess I've made. "I'm so sorry, Mrs. M. I am so, so sorry."

Massey and Briggs laugh hysterically as Chris carefully strips off his sneakers and Mrs. Massey descends on us with a roll of paper towels.

"Don't worry about this, dear," she says, shooting me a knowing glance. "Sometimes these things can get messy."

Chapter
THIRTY-SEVEN

Messy is one way to put it. Confusing is another. Or disturbing, terrifying, mortifying, thrilling.

For the next two days, Chris and I avoid making eye contact. What happened on that staircase? Did we seriously almost kiss? At night in my room, I close my eyes and relive the scene over and over, minus the unfortunate ending. I can practically feel the heat of his breath and smell the cottony scent of his t-shirt. I sense the strength of his hand in mine. Sometimes, when I'm not careful, I let my imagination wander further, and his lips press onto mine, soft and playful at first and then stronger, more eager, until—

That's where I stop myself. I can't go down that road. The whole thing happened so quickly; I'm not sure where it was going. And even if we had kissed, it's possible—

maybe probable—that Chris would have regretted it. That things would be even more awkward between us now. Not to mention, I would have betrayed Lindsay in the worst possible way. For all my talk about ethics and responsibilities and loyalty, I was ready to jump at the first chance I had to kiss a client's BF. What does that say about me?

The worst part is that I can't talk to anyone. Abi is the only person I can confide in about Chris, and she hasn't said a word to me since our disaster of a meeting. I've decided I need to make things up to her, which is precisely why I find myself Tuesday evening at the courts down at Claymore Park, purposely losing to Briggs at what has to be the longest game of HORSE in the history of mankind.

"Oh, man. I'm off today." I feign disappointment as my fourth attempt at an "S" shot caroms off the backboard. Not that I'm counting.

"Must be your jacket. It's cursed." Briggs motions toward my new jean jacket, draped across a bench. I probably shouldn't have brought it since I'm trying to butter him up, but hey, a girl can only tamp down her pride so far.

"Hah! That's game." Briggs gives me a huge smile as his "E" shot drops through the hoop. Finally.

"Nice one." I reach out to shake his hand. "Good game. How about we swing by Italiano's and I'll by you a slice as your reward?" If free pizza doesn't win him over, nothing will.

Briggs eyes me warily. "With pepperoni?"

"Sure. Whatever you want. Why are you looking a gift HORSE pizza in the mouth?"

He waves his hand at me. "You're up to something. It's not like you to be so nice about losing."

I slap his hand down. "You mean it's not like me to lose. When I do, I keep it classy."

"Right." Briggs appears unconvinced, but he follows me in his car to Italiano's, where we order our slices at the counter and pour our drinks. I grab a hundred napkins—because I've seen Briggs eat pizza before—and pick out a quiet booth near the back. My stomach is in knots. As much matchmaking as I've done over the past six months, I've never done it in person. What if I screw this up?

Briggs sits down across from me, a huge smile on his face. "So. Did he kiss you?"

"What?" I spit out my mouthful of Diet Coke and proceed to choke.

"Whoa, Lexi, chill out." Briggs grabs some of the napkins and wipes up the table. "What's your problem? Is that a yes?"

I cough out my answer. "What's *your* problem? Why would you ask me that?"

"Forget it, dude. I just figured … you hired the freaking Boyfriend Whisperer to get him, and you showed up at that party together, so—"

"Oh, you mean Jerod!" I take a deep breath.

Briggs looks at me like I'm crazy. "Yes, Jerod. Who did you think I meant?"

"Nothing. I mean, no one. Of course you meant Jerod. And no, he didn't kiss me."

"He didn't?"

"No. Not that it's any of your business."

"Did you want him to kiss you?"

"What? Why do you care? And isn't that kind of a …" I wave my hands in the air. "I don't know. A girly thing to ask?"

Briggs shrugs. "I'm a romantic. What can I say?"

"You? A romantic."

"Sure. Why not?"

"Try playboy." This is more like it. I need this conversation to be about him and Abi, not me and my ridiculously screwed up love life.

"Tomato and black olives?" The Italiano's server appears by our table with a slice in each hand.

"That's mine." I tap my placemat and thank her.

"So then, you must be the pepperoni." She offers Briggs a huge smile and sets his plate down with a flourish. "That's my favorite, too. Probably not the healthiest choice, but …" She giggles and touches his arm.

"It has tomato sauce on it," Briggs says. "Tomato is a vegetable. Therefore, it's healthy."

"I like the way you think." She gives his arm a squeeze and heads back to the kitchen, her hips a-swishing.

I kick Briggs under the table. "See? That's what I'm talking about."

"What?"

"That. You flirt with every girl you meet."

His eyes widen. "I wasn't flirting. I was merely offering a nutritional opinion. If anyone was flirting, it was her."

"Okay. Maybe she was flirting, but that doesn't mean you had to flirt back."

"I told you, I wasn't." He leans forward and lowers his

voice. "Can I help it if girls throw themselves at me? I'm a living, breathing chick magnet. It's like flies to a flame."

"You mean moths. Or honey."

"What?"

"Nothing. Never mind." I sigh and take a bite of my pizza. Briggs is right, but that doesn't make it any less maddening. I mean, come on. I was sitting right here. What if I were his girlfriend? I felt disrespected, and I don't even like Briggs. I can see how it got old for Abi. Still, she's miserable without him, and if I can make this happen, maybe she'll go back to talking to me. Or at least whining. At this point, I'd welcome the whining. I take a deep breath. "So, who are you taking to prom?" I try to sound casual.

Briggs shrugs and answers through a full mouth. "I dunno."

"You mean you haven't asked anyone yet?"

"Nobody I want to ask."

"No one?"

"Nope."

"I think there is someone. I think you want to ask Abi, but you're too chicken."

He scowls. "That ain't it."

"What then?"

Briggs's face softens and his shoulders sag. "What would be the point? She'd say no. Why should I put myself through that?"

I'm tempted to point out that his reasoning and being "too chicken" amount to the same thing, but something about the strain in his voice stops me. Instead, I shake my head. "You don't know that."

"Yes, I do. She won't take my calls, won't even look at me in the hallway. You think she's going to agree to spend a whole night with me at some stupid dance?"

"Maybe. If you ask her the right way."

"You mean, like, with flowers or something?" He rolls his eyes. "Now who's being girly?"

"Um. Hello? First of all, I'm a girl." Why was that so hard for people to grasp? "Second of all, though flowers would, in fact, make a lovely gesture, that's not what I had in mind."

"What then?" Briggs eyes me suspiciously. "You're up to something, Malloy. What is it?"

I lean forward and smile. "Only the best promposal idea ever."

Chapter
THIRTY-EIGHT

The line for popcorn stretches half the length of the lobby. I check my phone. Jerod and I have plenty of time before the movie. "Hungry?"

"Are you?" Jerod looks surprised, perhaps because we just ate a huge dinner at Sweetwater, including an extra basket of their Ozzie rolls, which amounted to six rolls in all, of which I ate five, and he ate one, not that I was counting.

This is our second date, but it's our first real date, and in fact it's my first ever dinner-and-a-movie date with a boy. I want to do it right. Also—not that this has anything to do with anything— but Chris is working behind the snacks counter.

I edge toward the line. "I'm not starving, but that popcorn smells yummy, don't you think?"

Jerod rolls his eyes and follows me. "Children are starving in Sudan while half of Loudoun County lines up to pay seven dollars for bags of popped corn smothered with partially hydrogenated butter-flavored oils. Nutritional value, zero."

I force a smile and point a finger in the air. "Great source of fiber, though."

This is how the entire evening has gone. Turns out, Jerod is a major health nut, not to mention uber socially and politically conscious—not that there's anything wrong with that. I like an occasional GMO-free salad as much as the next girl, though I could have done without the grimace when I ordered the bacon burger. Still, he's been super sweet, and we did have fun reminiscing about the good old days of getting up at o-dark-thirty for warm-up laps at camp.

I peek at Chris as we inch closer in line, but he's swamped and doesn't notice us. He and I haven't talked much since the Almost Kiss—if that is in fact what it was. We were forced to interact during chem lab on Thursday, where we exchanged a few pleasantries, including, "Can you pass me that vial?" "Do you have the iodine?" And my personal favorite, "Is there something wrong with this Bunsen burner?"

Awkward, awkward, awkward. On second thought, maybe this popcorn idea wasn't so brilliant after all. Sure, it was my idea to come to the movies, and yes, I knew Chris would be working, and in fact, it may have crossed my mind that we might run into him. My stomach lurches, and I eye the door to the theaters. If we get out of line now, he may never know we were here.

"Can I help the next in line?" Chris glances up from the cash register, his eyes meeting mine.

Wait. What? How did we get to the front already? I blink, and my brain considers a shrieking escape toward the exit, but my mouth somehow manages to spit out, "Popcorn."

"Oh, hey. Lexi. What are you—" His face darkens as he spots Jerod behind me. "I see." He motions toward the display behind him, his voice flat and cold. "Small, medium, or large?"

"Small," Jerod pipes in. "And skip the faux-butter."

Chris says nothing, but his eyebrows shoot up. He knows I love my butter. I busy myself with my wallet. "I've got this, Jerod. You bought the tickets."

Jerod and I argue back and forth about who will pay while Chris watches through hardened eyes. I shove a ten across the counter, ending the argument.

"We had dinner at Sweetwater." I'm not sure why I feel the need to tell him this. Perhaps it's an apology for our anemic popcorn order, or perhaps it's because I want to drive home the fact that this is a full-on date. A real, straight-up, girl-and-boy date, and in case he still hasn't noticed, I'm the girl.

Chris fails to acknowledge my pronouncement. In fact, he refuses to look at me as he hands Jerod the popcorn. "Enjoy your movie."

Chapter
THIRTY-NINE

Dear Anita:

You're doing great. Honestly. Sometimes these things take a while. Please just try to stick with it. Your next step is as follows:

Tomorrow evening, show up at Pollo Delicioso at 7 p.m. and order some takeout. This is the end of Jose's shift. He usually walks home from work, but you will offer him a ride. On the way to his house, ask if he has any pets. He loves to talk about his Chihuahua, Taquito.

When you arrive at the house, tell him you'd like to meet Taquito. Hang out for a few minutes and play with him, and make sure to ask whether he knows any tricks. (He can shake, roll over, and dance. It's honestly the cutest thing.) After a while, tell Jose you wish you could stick around longer but you need to get the chicken home before it gets cold.

Do not initiate contact again until you receive my next email. Good luck. You've got this!

Sincerely,

The Boyfriend Whisperer

www.boyfriendwhispererenterprises.com

I close my eyes and hit "send." Never have I been less confident in my whispering abilities, and my three weeks is almost up. Since making the brownies, Anita has completed two other assignments. She got Jose to help her with her algebra homework and paired up with him as tennis partners during their gym class. She seriously has done a great job. But Jose and Maria are inseparable. They ride the bus together, eat lunch together, walk through the hallways holding hands together. And the worst part is, they're really, really sweet together.

I've failed only once in my career as the Boyfriend Whisperer, when Joletta Smith hired me to whisper Bryan Owens. I tried every trick in the book for those two, only to find out after three weeks that Bryan doesn't like girls. Not that way, anyway. Not much I could do but process Joletta's refund.

This time, though, is different. I need to try to make it work, for Anita's sake and, if I'm being honest, for mine. I need to know that just because a guy is going out with a girl and just because they seem like a great couple, it doesn't mean they're right for each other. The right girl could be waiting in the wings, and if she sticks with it long enough, things just might work out.

"A small popcorn?" Chris catches up with me at my locker first thing Monday morning. "That's the oldest trick in the book."

"What are you talking about?"

"Come on, Lexi. You're smarter than that. Why would a guy order a small popcorn for two people?"

I sigh. If you're Jerod, it's apparently because you have a moral objection to enjoying a delicious snack while watching a super-preachy documentary about how technology is ruining everyone's lives. But I don't tell Chris this. Instead, I rest my hands on my hips. "Why don't you enlighten me?"

Chris rolls his eyes. "You're sitting in a dark theater, side by side. How many times did he grab your hand when you both reached into that tiny bag? And at what point in the movie did he finally slip his arm around you?"

"Sounds like the voice of experience."

Chris's face grows red. The kids walking by have started to stare, so I take a step toward him and lower my voice. "Not that I have to answer to you, but for the record, Jerod did not have a single kernel of popcorn." I smile sweetly.

"Though he did grab my hand. If I recall correctly, it was sometime during the opening credits. And he didn't let it go until long after the movie ended."

The part about the popcorn is true. The part about Jerod grabbing my hand is not. In fact, I grabbed his halfway through the movie, and he seemed okay with it, but that's as far as things went. Much as I hate to admit it, his lack of game is starting to bother me. Sure, it's great to be respected, and I don't particularly want him jumping all over me, but a kiss might be nice. Or two. What if it's me? Maybe I'm not the kissable type.

"Hey, are you okay?" Chris touches my elbow, his eyes searching mine. I hate that he can see past my smile.

I pull back and nod. "I'm fine. Did you know that three out of five people spend more time with their computers than with the people they love?"

"What?"

"And thirty-eight percent of teens are harassed or bullied online."

"Um. Okay." Chris's eyes widen. "Wait a minute. Did he take you to see that tech-gone-bad movie? Are you kidding me?"

Suddenly I feel the need to defend the preachy documentary. "For your information, it was very informative and … educational," I say. "A movie doesn't have to have a chase scene to keep my attention."

With that, I slam my locker and waltz away. If I'm being honest, a chase scene or two would have done wonders for that movie.

Chapter
FORTY

Wednesday morning, I wake with a start. Today's the day. My mind buzzes the way it usually does before a big game, but this isn't about me. It's about Abi. If all goes according to plan, Operation Promposal will go down after the last bell.

Of course, that's a pretty big "if." Maybe I shouldn't have planned something quite so elaborate. My classes drag, and I squirm and fidget through them like a six-year-old, full of nervous energy. What if not everyone shows up? What if Abi doesn't arrive at the appointed location at the appointed time? What if someone blabs to her? Worst of all, what if Briggsy wusses out at the last minute?

Half the school is buzzing with anticipation, including Chris and Massey. "Who do you think is behind this?" Chris asks me as I sit down across from him at lunch.

I shrug. I swore Briggs to secrecy. Can't have the entire school catching on to my mad matchmaking skills. "Maybe he came up with it himself."

Chris and Massey laugh as though that's the funniest thing they've ever heard. Which perhaps it is. "Hey." Massey nudges Chris's arm. "Maybe there's a Girlfriend Whisperer out there somewhere."

"Maybe."

"I need to hook up with her. Or him. Maybe we should beat Briggs up until he tells us who it is."

"Ah, ah, ah." I wave a finger at them. "Violence."

Lindsay joins us, her eyes shining. "You guys, I'm so nervous. What if I can't stall Abi from getting to her locker this afternoon? Everything hinges on it, you know."

I should be thrilled that Lindsay is taking her role to heart. After all, she's right; everything does hinge on it. But instead, I'm annoyed that she's acting so important. After all, Abi is one of the most easily distracted people I know, and she only has to stall her for about five minutes. Part of me wants to show Lindsay up and proclaim to Chris and Massey and the whole stupid cafeteria that I, Lexi Malloy, am the mastermind behind today's production. Whereas just minutes ago, I wanted nothing more than to keep it a secret, now I'm dying to tell everyone. Of course, that would be rash and highly counterproductive, so instead, I glare at Lindsay and take a big bite of my mac and cheese as I swallow my pride.

The plan is true brilliance. Last fall our school did a production of *Grease*. A few days ago, I reached out anonymously to a few of the cast members and asked them to revise one of the numbers and perform a flash mob for Abi's benefit. Oh, yeah, and to teach Briggs some of the words and dance moves while they were at it. It should be entertaining, and, I hope, successful in showing Abi that she—and only she—is the one he wants.

Civics is my last class of the day and after about three hours, or maybe forty-five minutes, of listening to Mr. Grawley drone on about the importance of due process, the bell finally rings. I shoot out of my desk, through the door, and toward A Hall, where Abi's locker is located. By the time I reach it, most of the cast is already assembled. Roland Briggs, on the other hand, is nowhere to be seen.

"Where is he?" Marcus Winters, the guy who played Danny and presumably taught Briggsy everything he knows, is muttering and wringing his hands. "If he stands us up after all those hours trying to teach him a proper hip swivel, I swear I'll kill him." Marcus is a total drama king, and I swear I'd laugh if I weren't so annoyed at Briggs myself. I slip away and head toward the nearest boy's bathroom. It's worth a shot.

I knock on the door and crack it open. "Briggsy? You in here? Is anyone in here?"

Briggs appears at the door, his face pale and his eyes wide. "I can't do it, Lexi. I'm sorry, but I'm—"

I push my way in and shut the door behind me. "Briggsy, Briggsy, Briggsy. You can and will do this—right down to each and every hip swivel. Because you adore Abi, and you'd do anything for her, and anyway, if you really throw yourself into it, you'll be awesome. I get that you're nervous, but everyone will love it so long as you own it."

Briggs shakes his head. "That's not it. I don't care what people think. And anyway, believe it or not, I'm actually pretty good at the hip swivels." He performs one for me, and I have to admit, boy's got game.

"What then?"

"What if she says no?" His voice is strained. "What if after everything, Abi still refuses to go to prom with me?"

I blink. I'm used to delivering girl-power pep talks, but this is new. Could Briggsy—the self-proclaimed living, breathing chick magnet—have the same insecurities as some of my clients?

"Dude, she's not going to say no. Trust me. This will work." I check my Fitbit. "You have less than a minute before she arrives. Get your butt out there."

Briggs groans and punches the nearest sink. "Ow!"

"Brilliant." I grab him by the sleeve and pull him out the door. "Come on. If you don't ask her, you definitely will not be going to prom with her. What do you have to lose?"

Briggs rubs his hand and takes a deep breath. "You're sure she won't say no?"

I give him what I hope comes across as a confident smile. "I'm sure. You've got this."

Briggs follows me out the door and toward the still growing crowd. I slip away, so it doesn't look like we're together.

"There he is!" One of the girls rushes up to him and pulls him into place. "Remember your cue?"

Briggs glances over at me, and I give him a nod.

"Let's do it," he says.

A hush falls across the crowd as Lindsay and Abi appear

around the corner. Abi stops, her eyes wide. "What's going on? Why is everyone staring at me?"

A guy crouched behind Briggsy shouts, "Hit it," and the entire cast breaks into their adaptation of "You're the One that I Want." The girls throw themselves at Briggs, who brushes them off one by one as he stares at Abi, singing, "You're the one that I want, Abi. Ooh, ooh, ooh, Abi." At first, he's stiff as a statue, but on the second verse, he breaks out the hip swivels, sending the girls—and not just the rehearsed cast girls but pretty much every girl in the hallway—into a squealing mass.

Abi's expression is a mixture of amusement and horror. She glances at me, eyebrows raised. I shoot her a pleading look. *Say yes, Abi. Give him a chance.*

As the number ends, Briggsy takes a few running steps and drops to his knees, skidding across the tiles and stopping in front of her. He leans back and lifts his arms in the air. "Abi Eisenberg, will you accompany me to Grand View's Junior Prom?"

Abi looks from him, to me, to the crowd, and back to Briggs. Her voice shakes as she answers. "That was awesome, but I … I'm … I don't …" She turns and takes off down the hall.

Briggsy's shoulders slump. Everyone is dead silent, until a girl in the back giggles and stage whispers, "This is awkward."

Massey walks up to Briggs and punches him on the arm. "Tough one, dude. Sorry, but I gotta catch a bus."

With that, everyone disperses, leaving Briggs to wallow in his rejection. I want to run, but I can't. I got him into this mess, and I can't just abandon him. He peers up at me as I walk over. Where I expect to see anger, I see only defeat. Ugh. This is not the brash Briggsy I know and love.

I take off down the hall in the direction Abi ran. If she wanted to escape, I have an idea where she might be.

Chapter
FORTY-ONE

At first, I don't see her. Abi's crouched on the footstool, tucked behind a stack of paper towels.

"Hey." I pull up a box of tile cleaner and take a seat next to her. "You okay?"

"You shouldn't have done that." Her voice is low but controlled. At least she's not crying.

I say nothing. I was sure she'd love it. I thought she would be thanking me, not angry with me. I know I should apologize, but I'm not sure for what.

"I understand you meant well," she says finally. "But you put me in a bad position. Roland, too."

"Well, it wouldn't be a bad position if you'd said yes." I realize this is probably not a wise response, but I can't help myself. I grab her arm and plead with her. "Why didn't you, Abi? I know you like him. I know you want to go with him."

"It's not that simple."

"Right." I lean back, resting my head against the wall. "The thing is, I think he's learned. I honestly believe it will be different this time. You know he never meant you any disrespect, right? He was just kind of … clueless."

Abi turns to me, her expression guarded. "What if it's not different? What if I go back to him, and he turns around and does the same thing—flirting all the time and letting other girls hang on him right in front of me? I deserve better."

"You do. You absolutely do." I sit up straight and look her in the eye. "I'm asking you to give Briggsy a chance. And I can't promise you he won't mess up, but I can promise you I'll be the first in line to whack him upside the head if he does."

That brings a small smile. "So you're going?"

"What?"

"To prom?"

"No. What? I can't—"

"Lexi, please." Abi grabs both my hands in hers. "I need you there. For moral support. And the head-whacking thing. Seriously, you have to go."

"If I do?"

"I'll give Roland a chance."

I sigh and close my eyes. "Done."

I hang up before the second ring. Crap. Jerod's going to see my number. Why did I hang up? And why doesn't this get any easier?

I hadn't planned to go to prom. I don't have a date, and I'm not exactly the go-anyway-and-hang-out-with-a-bunch-of-girlfriends type, seeing as I have no girlfriends per se. I had my entire evening mapped out, with a proper mix of mindless action movies, rocky road ice cream, and self-pity. And of course, I would check Instagram every ten minutes for pictures of Lindsay and Chris in all their red-dress-and-possibly-red-tie glory.

Now I have to activate Plan B: Jerod. I'm not proud of the fact that I think of him as Plan B, especially since that puts him below rocky road. The whole thing is unfair and ill-advised and possibly even a bit mean. But I promised Abi I'd go to prom, and Jerod is my best shot. Anyway, I'm probably overthinking it. It's a stupid dance. It's not like it means anything. Jerod's a friend, and people go to dances all the time with friends. I do like him, though maybe not the way he likes me. At least, I think he likes me that way, despite the fact that he hasn't even kissed me. And how screwed up is it that even though I don't really like him that way I'm annoyed he hasn't kissed me?

Ugh. I sit down on my bed and cradle my head in my arms. I'm definitely overthinking this whole thing. *Chill, Lexi. Time to do this.* I hit redial.

Jerod picks up on the first ring. "Hello, Lexi Malloy."

"Hey."

Jerod says nothing. Does he know what's coming?

"So. Remember when you told me how much you love

a good party?"

"Yes?"

"Well, there's another one coming up next weekend, and I'm not sure how good it will be, but it's kind of a … prom."

"I see."

"So?"

"So what?"

"Come on. Don't play dumb."

Jerod laughs. "Oh, no. I made it easy for you the first time. This time, you're on your own. If you're not going to hire a plane to write it out in the sky or post a video on YouTube or come to my house and hold up a charming hand-made poster outside my bedroom window, you're at least going to have to say the words."

Fair enough. I take a deep breath. "Why do people say you're a player?"

Wait. What? Did I seriously just ask him that? I squeeze my eyes shut. I've been wondering about it all week, but this probably was not the best timing for that question.

"Jerod? Are you there?"

"Yeah. Sorry. I, uh, wasn't expecting that."

"Of course not, and … I'm sorry. I didn't mean to put you on the spot, and if you prefer not to answer, that's okay, but I actually kind of would like to—"

"It was this girl, Lisa."

"Oh?"

"Man, I can't believe this stupid rumor made it all the way to Grand View. Who told you I was a player?"

I hesitate. No way am I ratting out Chris. He was just

looking out for me, after all. "I heard through the grapevine, I guess. I don't think it's all over the school or anything. So what about this Lisa chick?"

"She liked me last year, but I was ... let's just say, not that into her. She's kind of loud, and she smells like smoke. I don't know if that's because she smokes or if someone in her family smokes, but either way, I'm kind of sensitive to it, so I can hardly stand to be around her. Sometimes my eyes start to water and—"

"I got it. She liked you. You didn't like her, or the way she smelled. So?"

"So I was kind of dating this other girl, Maddie, and Lisa got jealous, I guess. She started telling everyone I was ... you know."

"A player?"

"No. I mean, yes, sort of. She started saying I was seeing her on the side. Cheating on Maddie. She came up with these elaborate stories, and everybody believed them."

"But you weren't."

"Of course not. I was brought up to respect girls. Besides, what with the smoke smell and all ..."

An image of Jerod fooling around with some girl while trying not to smell her pops into my mind, and I can't help but laugh.

"What's so funny?"

"Nothing. I'm sorry. It's not funny. It's terrible, and I'm sorry she did that to you, and I will do my best to make sure people at Grand View know it's a vicious, untrue rumor." Stupid as it may seem, knowing that Jerod is not a player makes me feel better about the fact that he hasn't kissed me yet. He's respecting me. That's it. Maybe I'm not unkissable after all.

"Now that that's cleared up," Jerod says, "wasn't there something else you wanted to ask me?"

Chapter
FORTY-TWO

"Wow. What's all this?"

Mom has set out her finest china, and Dad is holding a plate full of steaks.

"I told you she had no idea," Mom says. "These kids never read their emails anymore."

Dad sets the plate down and hugs me. "Congratulations, sweetheart."

"For what? What's going on?" My stomach churns. It's true that I haven't checked my Gmail account in a few days. Now that basketball season is over and Coach Reilly has stopped sending out her reminders, all I get is spam and solicitations from colleges. I have a feeling the huge smiles on both my parents' faces have something to do with the latter.

"We had to hear it from Coach Reilly. She sent us both a

very nice congratulatory email this afternoon." Mom raises her eyebrows at Dad, and I know she's silently chiding him for the rather unkind things he said about Coach after the championship game.

I steady myself against the nearest counter. "Hear what? Could someone please clue me in?"

"U Conn. University of Connecticut. Can you believe it?" Mom is practically bouncing with excitement. "It's a partial, so it's not a free ride, but hey … it's U Conn. Of course, we need to find out what their plans are."

"They're not going to start her," Dad says. "Too much talent in that sophomore class."

"Well, not as a freshman, of course. But if they don't foresee starting her in at least a few games by the time she's a sophomore, she might be better off at Tech or one of the other schools."

I consider pointing out that I'm standing right here in front of them and that it's extremely annoying when they start talking about me as though I'm invisible, but instead I sit down and busy myself with finding the smallest steak. I'm feeling a little queasy all of a sudden.

"We need to schedule a visit." Mom sits down across from me. "I was looking at flights for next weekend and—"

"I can't do next weekend. It's prom."

"I see." Mom slices open a baked potato and sends Dad a meaningful glance. "Hand me the sour cream, dear."

My face grows hot. I'll never look at sour cream the same way again. For the millionth time this week, I imagine Chris's hand in mine and picture his eyes, his lips. My stomach flutters as he leans toward me, his mouth closing in on mine.

"So you plan to go to prom?" Mom pulls me back to reality.

I sigh and roll my eyes. "There's that analytical mind we all know and love. Yes, I'm going to prom."

"Don't use that tone with your mother." Dad's voice is sharp.

I know I'm being a brat, so I shove a piece of steak in my mouth and stare into my plate, willing them both to leave me alone. I want to eat as quickly as possible and get back to my room. And think about that Almost Maybe Kiss again.

"Are you going with that Gerald fellow?"

"It's Jerod, Mom. J-E-R-O-D. And yes, I am going with him."

"Is this serious?"

I raise my eyebrows at my dad as if to say, *See what I'm dealing with here? Do you understand why I resort to sarcasm?* but his stoic expression tells me I'll receive no sympathy from his end of the table. I take a deep breath and swallow the comment I'm dying to make about dropping out of high school to get married and have babies. Instead, I force a smile. "It's prom. That's all. Girls and guys go to prom together."

And some girls go to prom with guys they're not that into because they need a freaking date and yes I know that makes me a terrible person so how about you leave me alone and let me finish my dinner in peace thank you very much.

Chapter
FORTY-THREE

Dear Anita:
   I regret to inform you that—

I lean back in my desk chair and groan. This is the fifth time in two days I've tried to compose this email. What can I say that will make her feel better? A million stupid clichés come to mind, but somehow I doubt Anita cares about all those other fish in the sea. There's only one she wants, and he's already been caught, hook, line, and sinker. Speaking of clichés.

The worst part is, she did everything perfectly. She followed each of my instructions to a T. A few days ago she even succeeded in getting herself and Jose locked in a storage room below the theater for two periods before Mr. Murphy found them and fixed the "broken" doorknob. It was an extreme measure, my last-ditch attempt to make something happen, but it didn't work. Nothing worked. I failed her, just as I've failed myself for the past six months.

I kick the leg of my desk, sending my Kobe Bryant bobblehead doll toppling to the floor. Nothing will make Anita feel better. It's Band-Aid ripping time.

> Dear Anita:
>
> I'm afraid it's over. I'm sorry I was unable to whisper Jose for you. Please know you did nothing wrong. It didn't work out, but I don't believe there is anything you could have done differently to change the outcome.
>
> I know this hurts. No doubt it will stop hurting someday, or at least hurt less, but that's probably not much consolation right now.
>
> Want to know a secret? I think I get how you feel. You feel as though someone has taken part of your heart—a part that you usually keep hidden and safe and protected so well that sometimes even you forget it's there—and they've thrown it against a wall. You wonder how you ever let such a thing happen, and you want to tuck it away again, deeper and farther and maybe forever. I get that. The pain is real, and it sucks.
>
> I also know this: You are a wonderful person—smart, pretty, funny, resourceful, and kind, and I understand you make a hella good brownie. I say all of this not to try to cheer you up, but because it's true and because even though it might not seem like it right now, it's important.

Really important.

Thank you for placing your trust in Boyfriend Whisperer Enterprises. Please see Abi Eisenberg Monday morning and she will provide a full refund.

All the best,

The Boyfriend Whisperer

Boyfriend Whisperer Enterprises

www.boyfriendwhispererenterprises.com

"This place is amazing. I can't believe you found it. And I can't believe your mom let you drive us all the way up here." Abi squeezes my arm as we survey a seemingly endless sea of satin, lace, rhinestones, and shimmer.

Actually, when I told my mom Abi and I were going dress shopping, I failed to mention the fact that Lila's Bridal Shop and Formalwear is in Baltimore, almost two hours from Sterling. She no doubt would have insisted we go to one of the dozens of stores in Northern Virginia, which would have meant risking being seen by one of our classmates hanging out together. No way could I take that chance.

"Let's find yours first." Abi's eyes shine brightly. "Remember: open mind."

I brace myself and follow her toward a rack two-thirds of the way back in the store. I have no idea what distinguishes these dresses from all the others, but Abi seems to have a plan. My palms are so sweaty, I'm afraid to touch the delicate fabrics. I haven't worn a dress since the fourth grade, much less the heels, jewelry, and makeup Abi chattered about on the way here. What if I can't pull it off?

"This one seems pretty." I hold up a navy blue dress with a gray stripe across the top. "Though I don't know if I want to wear Pine Bridge's colors. Seems kind of disloyal."

Abi grins. "This is a dance, not a tournament. No one will be thinking about school colors. Still, that dress is all wrong for you. You need something sleeveless, to show off those amazing arms."

"I have amazing arms?"

"Um. Yes? Every girl at Grand View would kill to have your arms. You need a gown that reminds them of that."

Abi picks out dress after dress and helps me try them on. I feel ridiculous in all of them, but Abi insists I'll look great once I have the right shoes and accessories and hair. Of course, she's never seen me in heels. Pretty sure that'll amp up the ridiculousness factor by at least a power of ten.

Just as I'm about to pull an eeny-meeny-miny-mo on the huge pile of dresses we've amassed, Abi appears at the fitting room door with a silver strapless number. It's glittery and super fitted and has a slight mermaid thing going on at the bottom.

"Um. No. Put that back where you found it."

"Now, now. Open mind."

"I promised you I would go to prom. I didn't say I'd be the disco ball. I feel like I need sunglasses to be in the same room as that thing."

Abi purses her lips and shoves it toward me.

"Fine." I grab the gown from her. I'm tired and cranky and wish I'd never have to slither into another dress as long as I live. "I'll humor you. Then I'm going to close my eyes and point at that pile and buy whichever one my finger lands on."

I try to step into the dress but can't get it over my hips. "Oops. Doesn't fit."

"No worries," Abi says. "Slip it on over your head."

I glare at her as I step out of it and hand the dress back. "It's too fitted. No way am I wearing something this tight."

She offers a dramatic sigh as she takes the dress and starts to forcibly pull it over my head.

"What? Hey! What are you—" I flail blindly at her as she tugs the dress down over my face. Both of us topple into the pile of dresses, tulle prickling at my legs and arms and head as I try to surface for air.

Abi squeals, and a sharp rap sounds at the door.

"Ladies, may I help you?" The saleswoman's tone is sharp.

Abi and I look at each other, eyes wide, and she starts giggling uncontrollably.

"We're good," I manage. "Thank you."

We lay back into the dresses and laugh silently until I have tears streaming down my face and Abi is gasping for air. I'm still tangled up in the silver monstrosity, so she has to help me stand. She pulls it down over my shoulders and hips, shakes out the mermaid frills at the bottom, and steps back.

"Whoa."

"What?" I turn to the mirror and blink. Who's that rock star staring back at me?

Chapter

FORTY-FOUR

I stumble and grab onto the edge of my trophy case. Brilliant. If I don't twist an ankle in these things, perhaps I can break an arm or leg beneath an avalanche of trophies. Wouldn't Mom love that?

"You're doing fantastic," Abi assures me. "Keep your chin up and your focus ahead. Try not to think about it so much."

I wanted to buy flats, but she insisted on this stupid pair of strappy sandals with two-inch heels. Prom is a mere five nights away, and while everyone else will be hip-hopping around, I'll be trying to master the art of walking. I can see it now. At five-eleven, I'll tower above almost everyone in the room—a silver skyscraper careening precariously across the dance floor. I'll give the Wobble a whole new meaning.

"I can't wait to see Chris's face. He's going to love you in that dress."

"You mean Jerod."

Abi smirks. "If you say so."

"I do." I pace the length of the room and back again, as slow as a turtle through a pool of molasses at first but picking up speed as I go along. "Seriously, I refuse to spend the whole night thinking about Chris. First of all, it's not fair to Jerod. I'm already basically using him to go to prom for you. I won't diss him by trying to flirt with another guy while we're there. Whoa." I lean against my desk and sink into the chair. I slip off my left shoe and rub my toes. "Second of all, it wouldn't be fair to Chris. This is his Junior Prom, and he deserves to have fun. He doesn't need me making waves when he's there with someone he really likes." *Though maybe doesn't love.*

"And what about you? What's fair to you?"

I shrug. "Same. It's my Junior Prom, too. I intend to avoid drama."

"In that dress?" Abi grins. "Good luck."

A rap sounds at the door, and my dad's voice calls in to us. "Lexi, dinner's almost ready. Your friend is welcome to stay if she wants."

Abi smiles and shakes her head. We both know that wouldn't be wise. It's been months since Chris has stopped by unexpectedly for dinner—ever since Lindsay entered the picture—but it's not outside the realm of possibility. Wouldn't do to have Abi sitting at the table.

"Before you go, how did Anita seem this morning? Was she upset?"

Abi shrugs. "She seemed okay, actually. She was a little quiet, but then, she's not much of a talker. She told me to thank you for trying."

"She said that? How sweet. So she's not pissed?"

"Why would she be? We gave her money back."

"So?" I turn and lift my hair so Abi can unhook my dress. "A lot of good that'll do her Saturday night when she's sitting home dateless. Or worse, when she goes to prom alone and has to watch Jose dance with Maria all evening."

"Lexi, it happens."

I turn back to face her. "Not to my clients. My clients end up with boyfriends."

"When I broke up with Roland, the first thing you said to me was, 'A girl doesn't need a boy to be happy.'"

"It's true. She doesn't. We don't. I believe that, one hundred percent. But still … if a girl has a boy she likes, she'll be even happier with him."

"Maybe." Abi's tone is wistful. "Maybe not."

I give her a hug, which is kind of awkward because my dress is half falling off, so I let go quickly and step out of the gown. "It'll be different this time. You'll see."

"I hope you're right, but even if you're not, I want you to know I appreciate everything you've done. The whole *Grease* thing and agreeing to go to prom and … all of it. It means a lot to me."

"That's okay. You're going to pay me back Saturday afternoon, remember? With the hair and the makeup and the nails?"

"Definitely." Abi claps her hands together. "That's not payback; that's icing on the cake. I cannot wait to glam you up."

I pull on a pair of sweats and some slippers and we head downstairs. As we reach the landing, Abi gasps and turns to me. "I almost forgot. Did you hear the news?"

"What news?"

"About Ty and Alicea." She makes a slashing motion against her neck.

"They broke up? They can't do that. They're my biggest success story."

"They *were* your biggest success story. He ended it yesterday."

"Ugh." Less than a week before prom? Nice timing. "Weren't they up for Prom king and queen?"

Abi nods. "Apparently, they're both still planning to go, though not as a couple."

Oh, my. I follow her to the front door and see her out. "Sounds like there will be drama a-plenty," I call after her. "My dress will be the least of everyone's concerns."

I shut the door and lean back against it, a smile tugging at my lips. *Though perhaps I wouldn't mind if it created at least a little bit of a stir.*

Chapter
FORTY-FIVE

A pop quiz? No way. How was I supposed to review my lesson on the Electoral College when I had thirty-one prom dresses to try on? Not that I was counting.

Mr. Grawley flashes an evil grin as he passes the test sheets down the aisle. "Pens and pencils down until I say you can start." I swear he stares straight at me. "Some of you have seemed a bit distracted the past few weeks. We still have more than two months of school left and a lot to cover. This quiz will count for ten percent of your final grade."

A collective moan from the class reassures me I'm not the only one who doesn't understand how the electoral system works. Then again, my dad says it doesn't, so maybe this is some sort of trick lesson.

"Okay, class, you may begin."

I flip the page and skim the questions. Two multiple

choice and three essays. This sucks. I'll be lucky to get a D. I narrow the first multiple-choice question down to two possible answers, and as I eeny-meeny-miny-mo my way through the two options, a miracle happens. The fire alarm.

Sweet! My classmates and I jump out of our seats and rush toward the door as though flames are licking at our heels. Chris and I bump fists as Mr. Grawley scowls and yells at us to proceed in an orderly fashion. His attempt to sabotage our afternoon has been thwarted, and I can't help but flash a smile as I walk past him and into the hallway.

As we wind down the nearest staircase, I spot Carmella a few steps ahead of me. "Yo, Mel!" I call to her, and she waits for me. "We just got out of a pop quiz in civics. How about you?"

Carmella shakes her head. "I swear you are the luckiest person on earth. I had study hall, and I really needed it. I have a paper due sixth period that's only half finished."

"Ugh. Bummer." I know I'm supposed to stick with my class when we get outside, but I ditch them and sneak off with Carmella and the kids from her study hall. I've been meaning to talk with her to try to figure out whether she's a threat to reveal my email address, but it's been tough since we don't have any classes together. This is my chance.

As we line up in the parking lot, I try to assume a casual tone. "So, how's your sister doing these days?"

Carmella's eyebrows shoot up. "How did you know I had a sister?"

"What do you mean? Of course I know."

She grunts. "Aren't you full of surprises? I never thought you knew the first thing about me. Or any of us."

Whoa. Harsh. I avoid her eyes. Just because I don't get all up in their business doesn't mean I don't care about my teammates. They should know better. I'm the consummate team player. I pass the ball whenever they have a better shot. I cheer them on when they make free throws and rebounds. What's with the hostility?

"Yes. I do know you have a sister. Her name is Krista, she's on the volleyball team, and she has a killer serve."

Carmella nods. "She does."

See? A girl can be aloof without being a total snot. I grin at the memory of Chris saying, "aloof" over and over at Elana's party.

"What's so funny?" Carmella eyes me as though I'm losing it.

"Nothing. Sorry." I pull her aside. "Can I ask you something?" This fire drill isn't going to last forever. I need to get to the point.

"Sure? What's up?"

"Um, nothing really. I was just wondering, how is Krista?"

Carmella's eyes narrow. "She's fine. Why?"

"Oh, no reason. I suppose I'm … curious about her. And her team."

"Wait. Are you, like, interested?"

"Interested?"

"In my sister? 'Cause she's not like that."

"Oh. No! No, no, neither am I. I didn't mean curious like that. I meant … gosh. That's embarrassing." I laugh, but Carmella's expression darkens. "Not that … you know … if I were, I'm sure I'd be interested in your sister. She's very pretty." Gaahh. This conversation is so not going the way I'd hoped.

"Then what? Do you have some sort of problem with her? Are you two fighting or something? Because that's between you and Krista."

"No, no. We're not fighting. We barely know each other. I was merely—"

"Lexi!"

I turn to see Chris running toward me.

"Where'd you go?"

"I'm right here."

"Everyone's looking for you. Grawley's pissed. Says he's giving you a week's detention."

Wonderful. I turn back toward Carmella. "Never mind. I was just asking because I care about you and your sister. And all my teammates."

Chris grabs my arm and pulls me toward our class line. "What was that about?"

"Nothing. Thankfully." Carmella could not have seemed more genuinely clueless. No way has her sister asked for my email address. Assuming Krista and the volleyball team were my biggest threat, Boyfriend Whisperer Enterprises has nothing to fear. I take a deep breath, but my feeling of relief is short-lived. Mr. Grawley has spotted me through the crowd, and his Machiavellian grin is back.

"Miss Malloy. Well, well. What have you been up to?"

"She was searching for us," Chris answers before I can say a word. "She got separated from us on the staircase. She had no idea where we went."

"Indeed?" Mr. Grawley looks Chris up and down. It's clear he doubts someone could lose sight of his six-foot-three frame, even in a large crowd.

"Oh, yes, I was frantic," I say. "Total panic mode."

I slip into line before Mr. Grawley can question me any further, and Chris steps in behind me. "Don't ever do that again," he mutters.

"What? I needed to talk to Carmella."

"Lexi, I'm serious." His expression holds the same mixture of alarm and relief as it did that day in Virginia Beach after I finally let him know I was okay. He places his hand on my arm, softly, lightly, sending a thrill through me, straight to my core. "One minute you were right next to me, the next you were gone. I had no idea where you went. What if something happened to you?"

"Like what?" I sigh at the concern in his eyes and soften my tone. "It's a drill, not a real fire. Of course I'd be more careful during a fire."

"How did you know it was a drill? It could have been real."

"Did you see any flames? Or smoke? At no time were we in danger."

"It's a big school."

"So you think I would have run toward the part of the building that was burning if there was a fire? Come on, Chris. Give me some credit."

He pulls me into his chest in a hug that's an awkward mix of tender embrace and friendly bro hug. "I was worried about you; that's all."

"Okay. I'm sorry." I close my eyes and breathe him in. His t-shirt smells like a mix of soap and cedar. "I promise not to disappear on you again."

"Never?"

"Ever."

Chapter
FORTY-SIX

I hear a car door slam and peer out my bedroom window. It's Jerod, looking good in his black tux, crisp white shirt, and black tie. I close my eyes and try to dream up a butterfly in my stomach, an uptick in my heart rate, sweaty palms, anything at all, but it's no use. He doesn't make me swoon, much as I wish he did.

I stop and steal one last look in the mirror, marveling at Abi's magic. Somehow she's succeeded in applying a half gallon of makeup to my face without turning me into a circus clown. She gave me smoky eyes and prominent cheekbones and lips the color of ripe raspberries. She brushed temporary highlights into my hair and hooked me up with earrings that sparkle almost as much as the dress. If I could master the snooty expression, I'd pass for a supermodel. With better arms. I flex both biceps, striking my best warrior princess pose.

"You go, girl." Mom appears in my doorway with a smile on her face and tears in her eyes. "You look so beautiful. So grown up." She walks in and motions toward my hair, my gown, my shoes. "When did this all happen?"

Mom doesn't tear up often. In fact, the last time I saw her cry was four years ago, at my grandfather's funeral. I give her a hug. "Amazing what a little mascara can do, huh?"

Mom grabs one of my perfectly manicured hands and pulls me back to stand in front of the mirror. "It's more than that. It seems like yesterday your dad was lifting you onto his shoulders to shoot baskets. Now you're taller than me, even without those heels." She lowers her voice and offers a conspiratorial smile. "Your date's cute."

"Isn't he?"

"You never did tell me how serious you are about him."

I give a slight shrug. "Jerod's awesome."

"That wasn't the question."

"Well, that's the answer."

Mom sighs. "You know, you'll probably laugh, but I always thought maybe you and Chris …"

I feel my cheeks flush, so I turn away. "That's crazy. We've been friends forever. *And* he has a girlfriend."

"Friends make great boyfriends. You know, your dad and I—"

"Yes, I do know." I've heard the story many times. They were friends for about eight months before they realized they were in love and started dating. One big difference between their situation and mine—they both felt it. Sort of needs to be mutual that way.

"Well, what you may not know is how frightened I was."

"You? Frightened?"

"Terrified. I didn't want to ruin a good thing. What if he didn't feel the same way? And even if he did, what if we got together and it didn't work out? What would happen to our friendship? The risks were very, very high."

"Yes, but the potential reward …" I make a circling motion around my supermodel face.

"I know. You're right." She laughs. "I hate to admit it, but you might not be here if your father hadn't made the first move. I couldn't do it. Wouldn't do it. I was too chicken."

This is a part of the story I've never heard. "So how *did* he make the first move?"

"Oh …" Mom offers a vague wave of her hand. "Suffice it to say it involved a darts lesson and a six-pack of beer. Not much to tell, really."

I have a feeling there is a lot to tell, but I also have a feeling I don't want to hear it.

"Speaking of your dad, shall we go save Jerod from him?"

I take a deep breath and nod. "Let's."

She grabs my hand and pulls me toward the door. "You look beautiful, sweetheart. You're going to knock them dead."

Or at least speechless. I'm not sure whose jaw drops farther when I make my entrance, Jerod's or my dad's.

"Smokin'." Jerod whispers it under his breath and then immediately backs away from my father.

Dad clasps his shoulder and pulls him back. "That's

all right, son. Just keep in mind that where there's smoke, there's fire. And smart boys don't mess with fire."

"Yes, sir." Jerod's eyes are so wide; I can't help but laugh.

"Stop it, you two." I wave them off but twirl around to make sure they get the full effect.

Mom pulls out her camera, and we pose for the obligatory prom shots. Finally, after the nineteenth photo—not that I'm counting—I cut her off. "You ready to roll?" I ask Jerod.

"Are you?"

"I am."

Grand View Junior Prom, here we come.

Chapter
FORTY-SEVEN

Chris's tie is black. Sweet. I can't help but give a small fist pump when I see it. He's posing for photos with a bunch of his teammates and their dates in a courtyard outside the ballroom, and his beautiful smile sends me swooning in my heels. I tighten my grip on Jerod's arm to keep from melting into a pool of silver across the floor.

Mid-shot, Chris glances over and spots me. His eyes grow wide, and his smile morphs into an expression of shock. Would love to get a copy of that photo.

"Wow." Massey whistles, and he and Briggs rush over to us. "Look at you, Malloy. You have a fairy godmother you never told us about?"

Briggs circles me and reaches out to touch a sparkle on my waist. "That dress is hot."

I slap at his hand. "Not as hot as Abi's, I'm sure." Briggs

isn't flirting with me. We've never had that vibe, but I want to remind him to keep his hands to himself and his date tonight.

Abi is hanging back with the rest of the group, watching us with a huge grin. I raise one eyebrow and wink at her. *Thank you, fairy godmother.*

Chris strolls toward us with Lindsay at his heels. Her dress is the color of rubies, and her hair is piled high atop her head, a few stray tendrils curling down around her bare shoulders. Very elegant.

"Lexi. Jerod." Chris is as stiff as the collar of his white pleated shirt. He clears his throat and looks at his shoes, his hands, the ceiling, anywhere but at us. "You two going to Briggsy's after party?"

I laugh. "Planning ahead? How about we enjoy prom first?"

Lindsay clasps her blood-red nails around Chris's arm and gazes up at him. "Exactly what I said." She makes a swooping motion toward my dress. "You look gorgeous."

"You too." Kills me to say it, but she does. No matter. I promised myself I wouldn't spend tonight thinking about Chris. Time to accept that fact that he and Lindsay look amazing together and belong together and will no doubt go to the after party together and then have their own little after-after party together and—

I blink hard. "So. Shall we go in?" I take a deep breath and grab Jerod's hand. "See you two in there. Have fun tonight." I turn on my heel and lead the way toward the ballroom. Time to keep my promise and enjoy prom.

The ballroom is pulsing with a Nicki Minaj song. A few

of my classmates are hanging out in clumps near the tables waiting for dinner service to start. A few are chatting in the corner and sipping punch from elegant faux-crystal glasses, and a few are making half-hearted attempts to pull their friends out onto the dance floor.

But most are watching Alicea Springer.

Standing on a riser by the D.J. booth, her arms in the air and her eyes closed, Alicea is having her own private dance party. She dips and twirls and stomps and shakes. I've never seen anything quite like it. I walk up to my teammates Paige and April, who are staring, wide-eyed, mesmerized by the spectacle. "How long has this been going on?"

"For at least three songs," Paige whispers, as though she's afraid to break a spell. "Isn't she fantastic?"

"Is she trashed?"

"I don't think so," April says. "She's just … in her own world. Which appears to be more fun than ours."

I glance around for Ty Walker and spot him at the hors d'oeuvres table with some friends. He's laughing and joking and seems completely unfazed by the fact that his former girlfriend is making a spectacle of herself in front of the entire school. I guess it really is over between them.

As the night wears on, I take inventory of all my couples. There's lots of hand holding and slow dancing and flirty giggles. Jolene and Brendon need to get a room. And Amy Wellbourn—the freshman tuba player I set up with drummer Brent Bartkowski—positively glows as the two of them sway to an Adele song.

And then there's Anita. For the first half of the night, she keeps to herself and a few friends, but somewhere between the Whip and the Quan, she and Robbie Yother totally hook up. They're on each other like butter on bread, and Anita looks as though she's having a blast.

"Lexi!" Jerod shakes my shoulder. "Are you okay? Where have you been all night?"

"What do you mean? I've been right here." I know what he means, of course. Enough worrying about everyone else. "Come on. Let's dance." I grab his hand and lead him onto the floor. This is my prom, too. And if Anita can get over Jose Ramos in the span of two songs, maybe I can truly get past a certain crush on a certain guy who happens to have kissed a certain date at least six times tonight. Not that I've been counting.

Chapter
FORTY-EIGHT

Jerod can dance. We're not talking about the running man and the chest pop and all the usual stuff the other guys are doing. He pulls out a six-step, a windmill, and a Michael Jackson-worthy spot shimmy.

"Where have you been hiding him?" Carmella appears at my side, her eyes shining as we watch him do a semi-backflip with a crazy twist. "And what the heck was that move?"

"No idea."

"Maybe they should call it 'The Jerod.'"

He ends with a freaking turtle freeze—and that's all for the first song. Holy crap. Where was *this* guy during our dates?

As the next mix comes on, a bunch of guys and even a few girls challenge him, and pretty soon, the entire dance floor has formed a circle around him. Some of the kids are pretty good, and some are just goofing. Briggs hops in and does about twenty hip swivels—his new signature move. Abi is in hysterics, and I can tell she's having an awesome time.

About six minutes into the mix, as Jerod lands on his feet after a killer airflare, Chris strolls onto the floor. What the what? My boy does *not* dance. Ever. They stare at each other for a full five seconds before Chris pops into a planche, his arms holding him up like a gymnast on the pommel horse, his body straight as a board from his head to his feet. Whoa. Those biceps are for real. Not to mention the ab strength.

The two of them go at it, and while Chris doesn't know nearly as many moves as Jerod, his technique's pretty solid. When the heck did he learn to do all this? And what's up with him acting like a rooster at a cockfight? Showing off for Lindsay, no doubt.

The beat of the music pounds as they perform dueling break moves, one answering the other, kicking things up a notch on each turn. They're talking trash the whole time, but they're kidding. I think.

Carmella elbows me. "Is it me, or did this escalate really quickly?"

"My thoughts exactly."

Jerod pulls a six-turn UFO while Chris attempts a jackhammer. Both of them pop out of their move at the same time and—wham! Jerod's forehead smashes into Chris's nose, and both go down.

"Holy—" I rush over to Chris, who's flat on the floor,

blood pouring from his nose. "Are you okay?"

He sits up, grimacing. Lindsay reaches him soon after I do, and she's a squealing mess. Apparently, blood's not her thing. I help Chris up and someone brings us a handful of paper towels. That's when I look around and notice Jerod sitting on the floor, holding his head. He's watching me, and I can see it in his eyes. He knows. Ugh. I am the worst date ever.

"Want to dance?" Chris holds out his hand and nods toward the floor, crowded with couples swaying to an old Jason Mraz song. Jerod is still cleaning up in the guy's bathroom, and Lindsay is nowhere to be seen. This is a lot like I've imagined dozens of times over the past few days, except it's real, it's happening, and ... well, there's a huge bandage across Chris's nose and a dark red bloodstain on his collar.

"Sure." I take his hand and let him lead me onto the floor. "So, do you dance in the shower, too?"

"What?"

My face burns. "Sorry. That sounded less ... personal in my head. You told me you sing in the shower, and it turns out you have a great voice, and tonight I find out you can dance, too."

Now it's Chris's turn to blush. "Thanks. Though I'm

not as good as your boyfriend."

"He's not my boyfriend." I say it quickly, probably a little too quickly.

"No?"

"He's a friend who's a boy."

"You have lots of those. You don't invite them all to prom."

"True." There's only one I really wanted to invite. I change the subject. "I see you went with black."

"Black?"

"Your tie. It looks good."

"Oh, right. Thanks. I might have worn silver, you know."

"What?"

"I mean if I'd come with you. I mean—" He looks away and takes a deep breath. "I should say, if Lindsay had worn silver, I would have worn a silver tie. I can see myself in silver. Not red. Red's too … flashy. Not that you're not flashy," he adds quickly. "That dress is super flashy."

"Okaaay. Thank you? I guess."

"Yes. It's a compliment. I mean it in a good way. A perfect way." He tightens his grip on my waist.

I'm dying to press closer to him, to reach up and touch his chin, his cheek, his earlobe. I wouldn't have to reach far. Tonight I'm only a few inches shorter than him. "It's crazy to see me in a dress and heels, huh?"

He shrugs. "Not so crazy."

"Oh, come on."

"What?"

"You think it's crazy."

"I don't."

"You do. Maybe just a little?"

"Why?" Chris laughs. "Why would I think that?"

"Because. You don't see me as a girl."

Chris stops dancing so abruptly I collide into him and trip over his foot. He grabs me and steadies me, his face—his lips—inches from mine. "That is *not* true."

"But …" I whisper the word. I can hardly breathe with him so close.

"But what?"

"You said so."

Chris's expression grows serious. "What did I say?"

I pull away. "Never mind. It's nothing." I don't want to repeat what he said that night in Italiano's. Not now, not here. *Since when are you an expert on girls? It's almost like you think you are one.* I blink back the tears that threaten every time I remember that dagger to the heart. "I should go find Jerod. And I'm sure Lindsay's looking for you."

But Chris doesn't let go. He spins me farther onto the dance floor. "Not until Jason is done singing."

I sway in his arms, and for the first time, I pay attention to the words of the song. It's about not giving up on love and figuring things out. With Chris's arms circling my waist and his chin grazing my cheek, I almost believe that's possible.

Chapter
FORTY-NINE

We can hear the band from half a block away. "Wow, that's loud," Jerod says. "Bet the cops show up before the night's over."

We pull up and watch as a crowd of kids spill out of Briggsy's front door. "We don't have to do this. Your head's already hurting. The death metal won't help."

"I'm fine," Jerod insists for the millionth time. "Don't worry about me."

We head in and weave our way through the sea of partiers to the kitchen, where we rummage through a cooler for drinks. Jolene and Brendon are standing in a corner by the refrigerator talking, or rather, shouting, since that's the only way to communicate. Brendon seems angry. He's saying something about the band, but I don't have time to process what's happening with them, because no sooner do I grab myself a bottle of water than Abi appears at my elbow, her eyes wide and her expression slightly panicked.

She grabs both my arms and leans in to scream into my ear. "You need to get upstairs."

"What? Why?"

"Just go. Second bedroom on the left."

"Second? Isn't that—" Crap. It's Briggsy's room. What's going on? Is he up there with another girl? Abi disappears before I can ask, so I hand Jerod the bottle of water and tell him I'll be right back.

I want to take the stairs two at a time, but it's impossible in heels and a gown. Instead, I clomp up them as quickly as possible, muttering under my breath the entire way about how hard I'm going to clip Roland Michael Briggs on the side of his big fat stupid head and how I'm going to give whichever twit he happens to be messing with up there an earful. I hit the landing and push my way through a group of girls waiting in line to use the bathroom and barrel toward Briggsy's room. I consider knocking but decide that's better than he deserves, so I fling open the door and— "Oh, my gosh!"

"Ack! You should've locked the door!" A half-naked Lindsay glares at me from the bed as a guy in a black tux hovers over her.

"Wrong room. I'm so sorry." I shield my eyes because I seriously do not want to see Chris's face at this moment, but as I back out and pull the door shut, I turn to spot a tall guy with blond hair rounding the corner at the other end of the hallway. I blink and take off after him. "Chris?"

He swivels, and I practically run into him as I turn the

corner. "Hey, Lexi." He frowns. "Are you okay? You look like you've seen a ghost."

"I … um. No. I mean, yes. I'm fine. How are you?"

His brow furrows. "I'm good. I was looking for Lindsay. Have you seen her?"

"Lindsay? No. Can't say that I have." I assume what I hope is an expression of innocence. "I'd know if I saw her. I mean, who could miss her with that red dress and all?" I grab Chris's arm and pull him down the hallway, past the offending bedroom door, and down the stairs. "I bet she's in the kitchen or the den or … have you checked the basement? I heard some kids are down there playing that Dance Revolution game. I bet she's really good at that."

I practically push Chris toward the basement door and slip away to find Abi. What the heck is going on? Who is Lindsay with?

I'm taller than almost everyone in the room, so I quickly spot her standing by the fireplace with Briggs. I catch her eye and hold up my phone. As she digs her cell out of her pocket, I text her to meet me in the garage. On my way there, I catch a glimpse of Carmella and Jerod talking and laughing in the dining room. She has her hand on his arm. Part of me is annoyed that Carmella is so obviously moving in on my date, but the other part of me is relieved that Jerod might find someone who appreciates him. I might feel less guilty about this whole night. Not that I deserve to.

"Can you believe it?" Abi bursts through the door and launches herself at me. She grabs my hands in hers. "I told you she's a lying wench."

"Hold up. Tell me what's going on."

"You mean you didn't see them?"

"I saw Lindsay. In fact, I saw way more of Lindsay than I needed to. But I couldn't tell who the guy was."

Abi glances around, making sure we're alone. "Ty Walker."

Chapter
FIFTY

Neither Ty nor Alicea won prom king or queen, but they both seemed to have a blast tonight. Alicea was out on the dance floor—sometimes with guys, sometimes with girls, and sometimes by herself—all evening long, and Ty had a grin on his face every time I saw him. Though come to think of it, I didn't see him much. He disappeared a lot, and so did Lindsay.

"Are you going to tell Chris about this?" Abi asks.

I lean against Briggsy's mom's Lexus. "I don't know. No. I can't. I think he really likes her."

"He deserves to know. She's making a fool of him. Half the party knows exactly what's going on."

I squeeze my eyes shut. How could Lindsay do this? It's stupid, but I feel a bit betrayed myself. I set her up with a guy—a sweet, gorgeous, amazing, incredible guy—

and she cheats on him in front of the whole school on freaking prom night. A dozen images flash through my mind: Chris's awkwardness in front of Lindsay in Virginia Beach, his smile as he held out that beautiful bouquet of roses on Valentine's, the two of them kissing at the lunch table, Chris chiding me that night at Joe's about what a nice person Lindsay is, her coy smile as she confided in me at the bowling alley.

I clutch my stomach. "I'm going to be sick." I push past Abi, running back into the house and toward the nearest bathroom. It's locked, and there's a line, so I turn around and bolt through the kitchen onto Briggsy's deck. I run to the corner of the deck, lean over the side, and hurl. Gross. I spit a few times to get the taste out of my mouth, then crouch down and hug my knees. I rest my head against the wooden railing. It's cool and hard and feels good against my burning skin. There are a few kids hanging out at the other end of the deck, but otherwise; it's empty. Thank goodness. I need some time to think.

What should I do? Abi's right. Chris does deserve to know, but I don't want to be the one to hurt him. On the other hand, it would probably be better if he finds out from a friend rather than through the grapevine. And I can't help but feel a little responsible for all of this since I set them up in the first place.

As I'm contemplating all of this, two girls from the cheer squad come out onto the deck. They're both drunk and are holding each other up. They stumble over to a nearby table and sit down. I should probably stand up or cough or say something so they know I'm here, but instead,

I sink farther into the shadows. I don't need them to see me in all of my post-puking glory.

"She finally did it," one of them says. "She's been after him forever."

"I know." The other girl pulls out a pack of cigarettes and fumbles to light one. "I do feel bad for Chris, though. He seems like a nice guy."

I bite my lip and steady my breathing. So Lindsay's tryst truly is the talk of the party.

"He's sweet, but I don't think she even liked him. She was always so hot and cold with him. She called him a revenge date, whatever that means."

"It means she was trying to get back at someone by dating him," says the smoker.

"I know that. But who? As far as I know, Chris never had a girlfriend."

The girl shrugs and blows out a long stream of smoke. "Who knows? Probably someone who has a crush on him. One thing's for sure. No matter how much she wanted revenge, she'll dump him now that she has Ty." She snuffs out her cigarette and rubs her arms. "It's freaking freezing out here. Let's get back inside."

The two of them scramble to their feet and go back in. I hadn't noticed the cold before Smoker Girl mentioned it, but now I rub at the goosebumps on my arms. What was that all about? Revenge date? For real?

I close my eyes and bury my head in my hands. They said she was hot and cold with Chris, but I never saw that. She was all over him whenever I was around, and—

Oh, no. No, no, no. Once again, I replay in my head

scenes of Chris and Lindsay over the past two months. The way she always grabbed onto his arm as soon as I'd walk up to them in the hallway and how she'd make a point of kissing him on her way past our chem lab table. One day when I came into class behind her, I noticed that she walked right past him and then circled back around after I sat down. Could that all have been a show for my benefit? And if so, why? Lindsay and I had zero contact before she started dating Chris. Why on earth would she want revenge against me?

Chapter
FIFTY-ONE

Hell hath no fury like a woman scorned, or so my sophomore-year English lit teacher said. I don't know whether Jolene has been scorned, but she's certainly furious. The glass she throws at Brendon narrowly misses my head as I walk back into the kitchen. It shatters against the doorjamb as Brendon pushes past me, out onto the deck, down the steps, and away into the night.

"What the—" I duck for cover behind the kitchen's center island as Jolene pulls a cast iron skillet out of the cabinet. "Whoa. Whoa. He's gone." I peek up at her and motion for her to set the pan down.

"That idiot." She slams the pan against the counter.

"Hey, yo. What's going on here?" Briggs appears in the doorway and surveys the scene. "What broke?"

"A glass," I straighten up and shoo him out of the room.

"Go find a dust pan. We'll clean it up. No worries."

As Briggsy leaves, I walk toward Jolene, slowly, carefully, as one might approach a seething tiger. I ease the skillet out of her clutches and push it to the back of the counter. "Tell me what happened."

Her eyes flash. "He called me a liar. A fake. All because of some stupid song."

"A song?"

"That noise the band was making earlier? Apparently, it was a cover of some 'iconic' metal song." She makes air quotes as she says "iconic."

"Okay?"

"I'd never heard it before and had no clue who the original artist was. Frankly, I couldn't care less. Problem is, he thought I knew my metal. He says I've been lying to him. Says I got him to go out with me under 'false pretenses.'" Again with the air quotes.

"That's not false pretenses. That's showing an interest in the things he likes. It's called flirting."

"That's not how he sees it. He says he fell for someone else." Her voice cracks. "Guess he never liked me for me."

I put my arms around her and rub her back. "Well then, he doesn't know what he's missing. Because, girlfriend, you are smart and beautiful and brave."

"You know whose fault this is? It's that stupid Boyfriend Whisperer." Jolene pulls away from me. "If it weren't for her, all this never would have happened. She's the one who told me to say all that stuff about metal bands and video games and things I know nothing about."

"Oh, well ... I don't know if you should blame her."

I force a casual tone. "After all, she's trying to help, right? It's her job. You hire her to whisper the guy, and she does whatever it takes to make it happen. Ultimately, you get the boy you want. It's the end result that counts, isn't it?"

"Yeah, well, this is the end result." Jolene points to the broken glass scattered across the floor. "Two months of my life wasted, not to mention the hundred twenty-five dollars I paid her, and another three hundred for this dress and the shoes and the prom tickets. Ugh! What a scam. What a freaking scam! If I ever find out who she is, I'll—"

"Did someone ask for a dust pan?" Abi appears in the doorway, a pan and sweeper in hand.

"You!" Jolene rushes Abi, pinning her against the wall. "You did this. You and your idiot boss."

"Hey, now." I pry her away from Abi. "Easy. She hasn't done anything to you."

"She took my money. She's part of the scam."

A small crowd has started to gather. The band is on break, so Jolene's ranting is now officially the loudest thing at the party. "Tell me who she is." Jolene is straining against my hold, her face inches from Abi's. "I want a name. Tell me who the Boyfriend Whisperer is."

Abi widens her eyes at me but doesn't say a word.

"Calm down, Jolene. You've had a stressful night. Things will look better in the morning. Besides, if Brendon doesn't appreciate you for you, he doesn't deserve you. There are lots of guys out there who will."

Ugh. Why am I suddenly spouting every breakup cliché in the book?

Jolene's eyes flash. "What do you know?" She reaches

up and grabs a lock of my hair. "Miss Super Star. You have it all—beauty, brains, talent. A free ride to any college you want. You have no idea what it's like for us mere mortals." She tugs at my hair.

"Ouch. Stop it. What are you even—"

At that moment, both Chris and Jerod arrive at my side, pulling Jolene away. I blink back tears, partly from the pain of having my hair pulled but mostly from shock at what Jolene said. Is that really what she thinks? Is that what everyone thinks? That I have it all? Because it sure as heck doesn't feel that way to me. I look at Chris, so gorgeous in his tux, his cowlick starting to show despite his spiking gel. I don't have the thing I want most.

"What's going on?" Lindsay appears in the doorway with Ty. Her perfectly styled hair is now a mess around her shoulders, and a dark spot is starting to form about two inches above her collarbone. Seriously? She's not even going to pretend to be a decent human being? Guess Jolene and Brendon is not the only break-up going down tonight.

"Lindsay, I've been looking everywhere for ..." Chris's face darkens as he notices Ty's hand on her arm. I can see the realization sinking in, and it makes me want to do to Lindsay what Jolene was about to do to Abi. My stomach twists. I should have told Chris right away what was happening. It would have sucked, but it would have been a lot better than watching him humiliated in front of everyone like this.

"I'll tell you what this is about." Jolene pulls away from Chris and Jerod. Whether she is oblivious to the new source of drama that has entered the room or is simply determined to keep center stage, I'm not sure. "This is about a vicious scam that's been going on at our school, and we've all just gone along with it. We've even encouraged it. This is about the Boyfriend Whisperer, who's been playing us for fools. She convinces us to tell guys what they want to hear as though that's the secret to love, without a care for what happens when they find out it was all an act. She's a fraud and a thief, and I want to know who she is."

"Well, that's simple," Lindsay says as she turns her gaze toward me and smirks. "You're standing right beside her."

Chapter
FIFTY-TWO

No. Way. Did Lindsay just out me to the entire school? I barely have time to process the implications of what's happened, because Jolene lets out an ear-piercing shriek and rushes me again. I step away, and my heel catches on the swirl of fabric at the bottom of my dress. I tumble backward as though in slow motion, and I'd land flat on my butt if it weren't for Abi, who reaches out and breaks my fall. Everyone else steps away as though I'm some sort of pariah.

Chris, Jerod, and Briggsy all grab onto Jolene and hold her off. The three of them can barely contain her. "I want my money back!" she screams, arms flailing wildly. "I want my money back, and my prom, and the last two months of my life!"

"How about your dignity?" Abi mumbles, and it's all I

can do not to laugh in spite of the horror show unfolding around me.

As Hurricane Jolene loses her strength, Jerod releases his grip on her arms and steps over to me. "What is she talking about? What's the Boyfriend Whisperer?"

I survey the sea of faces staring at me, including so many couples I've brought together. The girls seem nervous I might reveal their secrets, and the guys are eyeing me warily.

"I'll tell you what it is." Lindsay steps forward, still smirking like a cat toying with its prey. "It's the silliest thing, really. Girls pay her to help them get a boy. Think about it. What kind of loser needs to pay money to get a date? Not to mention, her methods are juvenile, at best. She basically snoops around the guy's life and feeds a bunch of useless trivia to her clients." She glances at Chris. "Things like their favorite basketball team."

She makes a sweeping motion toward the crowd. "It's unbelievable how many of you have fallen for it."

And then it happens. It starts with murmured whispers and suspicious stares and escalates to arguments and accusations.

"Did you figure out that Dead Rising hack by yourself or did you Google it?"

"If I took you out on a boat right now, would you have any idea how to actually bait a hook?"

"Have you ever even seen any of the Mad Max movies?"

As guys begin to shout, and girls begin to protest, several of the couples turn their wrath toward me. They're calling me names and screaming and pointing as though

I'm some sort of criminal. If someone had a stake and matches handy, I'd be toast.

"We should go." Jerod grabs my arm, eyeing the angry mob in all their shimmery, glittery, lacy glory. "This can't end well."

"No. It's not fair." I pull away from him. "Let me explain." I try to shout above the ruckus. "I was trying to help. I just want you all to be happy and find love."

But it's no use. Everyone is shouting me down, and they're starting to press in on me. Again Jerod grabs my arm, and he pulls me toward the door. "Prom night's over."

As we reach the front porch, I glance back past the fighting couples, the classmates calling for my head, and Lindsay's triumphant glare to catch a glimpse of Chris's face. He's pissed. And hurt. And generally looks as though he never wants to see me again.

Chapter
FIFTY-THREE

I wake up Sunday morning feeling hung over, though I never had a drink, and my back feels the way it did the time Massey mowed me down on his way to the basket in the ninth grade. Must have pulled something when I tripped over my dress. I pull a pillow over my head and moan.

How did everything get so screwed up so quickly? How can I face everyone at school tomorrow? What am I supposed to do with my life now that Boyfriend Whisperer Enterprises is the most vilified startup on the planet? And what will I say to Chris the next time I see him?

My phone buzzes.

It's Abi, no doubt calling to point out that this is my fault and that we should have quit while we were ahead. I consider not answering, but I know I've made things tough for her. I owe it to her to let her rant. I squeeze my eyes shut and answer. "Hey, chica."

"You okay?" Her voice is soft and gentle, not at all what I'm expecting. For some reason, this makes me feel worse.

"No. You?"

"I'm sorry about last night."

"Not your fault, obviously. Anyway, I'm sorry too. About last night and about ... everything." My voice cracks. Jolene had Abi pinned against the wall, yet she revealed nothing, and when everyone else was content to watch me fall, she reached out and caught me. I've never given her enough credit. She's been the most loyal employee anyone could hope for. "I also should thank you. You had my back last night. I appreciate it."

Abi pauses. "That's what friends do."

Oh, man. Why did she have to go and say that? Tears spring to my eyes, and I grab the box of tissues from my nightstand. "I'm your boss, Abi. Or was. Now ..."

"Now we're friends. And to be honest, you're in no position to be picky. I may be the only friend you have at this point."

In spite of everything, this makes me smile. "Ah, yes. That's the Abi I know and love. Or at least, put up with."

"Actually, I take it back."

My heart sinks. Why do I always have to ruin everything? "Abi, I'm kidding. I know I haven't always been the nicest to you, but—"

"Shut up, silly. I don't take back being your friend. What I mean is, I take back saying I'm your *only* friend. Briggs is still your friend, too. We both know you meant well. And we both appreciate what you did for us. Twice."

I tear up again. She's right. The Boyfriend Whisperer hasn't been a complete failure. I brought those two together. Now if only I could convince the rest of my classmates.

As we hang up, my phone buzzes again. This time, it's Jerod. Crap. Just when I was starting to feel a little better about myself. He was such a sweetheart last night, and I was ... not.

I swipe to answer. "Thank you, and I'm sorry."

He laughs. "That's an interesting way to answer the phone."

"I mean it. I suck, and you're awesome, and you didn't deserve last night."

"It wasn't so bad. And it was probably a whole lot more exciting than my prom will be next weekend."

I tense up. Don't tell me he's about to ask me to his prom. That apology was about more than the after-prom party disaster. It was about the whole night. About asking him in the first place when actually I wanted to be there with Chris.

"You really like him, don't you?"

"What? Who?" What is he, some kind of mind reader?

"He's a stand-up dude. You could do worse."

I close my eyes. "I'm sorry, Jerod. You're such a great guy, and—"

"Lexi. I don't need the 'great guy' speech. It's okay. You and Chris belong together. Anyone can see that."

Right. Except for Chris. "Yeah, well. He hates me now, so that's not going to happen. But thanks for the vote of confidence."

"He'll come around. Guys have short memories when it comes to this kind of thing. Trust me."

I get the feeling Jerod has something else he wants to tell me, but what? Surely he didn't call me merely to deliver a pep talk about Chris.

He clears his throat. "So like I was saying, I have prom coming up next weekend."

Right. He *is* going to ask me to prom. And I can't very well say no when it's clear I asked him to mine for selfish reasons. Besides, I have the dress and shoes. I have no excuse.

"I was wondering if you'd mind if—"

"Sure. Not a problem. I owe you that much."

"But you don't even know what I was going to say."

"It's kind of obvious, isn't it?"

"I was going to ask if you'd mind if I took Carmella to my prom."

"Carmella?" I cover the phone and let out a sigh of relief. "I ... yeah, I kind of thought that's where you were going. And it's definitely not a problem. Go for it. You'll have an awesome time."

As we hang up, I smile. First Abi and Briggs, and now Jerod and Carmella. I didn't bring either couple together using my typical strategies, but I did bring them together. Maybe things aren't as bad as they seemed last night. Maybe Boyfriend Whisperer Enterprises still has a chance.

Chapter
FIFTY-FOUR

O r not. Monday at school, half of my couples have broken up, and the other half are arguing. My locker is a rainbow of graffiti and sticky notes—twenty-seven of them, not that I counted. My favorite is a little poem.

ODE TO A STUPID CUPID
You thought you were Cupid,
But really you were stupid.
I wanted to be Brett Bond's wife,
But instead, you ruined my life.
- Anonymous

Um. Okay. Since I only whispered Brett Bond for one client, I have a pretty good idea of who "Anonymous" might be.

The stares and the whispers are the worst. I hide in the F Hall janitor's closet for as much of the day as possible, scooting into my classes right as the bell rings and shooting out just as quickly. My social media has exploded, and not in a good way, so I avoid my phone.

During lunch period, I head to the closet with a Power Bar, a pear, and a juice box. As I round the corner at F Hall, I hear the click-clack of heels behind me. Lovely. Now I'm being stalked? As I walk casually past the closet, a shout stops me.

"Lexi!"

It's Abi. She's the first friendly face I've seen all day, and before I know what I'm doing, I hug her so tight she has to gasp for me to let her go.

"Sorry. I'm just … I … Abi, what am I going to do?" I tear up as she opens the closet door and shoos me in.

"I have to tell you something," she says, her expression serious. "Remember yesterday when I said I was sorry and you said this wasn't my fault? Well … it kind of is."

"What? What are you talking about? How can this be your fault?"

"I figured it out last night. How Lindsay found you out. It was me. Me and my stupid brother."

"Ari? What does he have to do with this?"

"That email thing I told you about. There's a reason he knew exactly how someone might figure out your identity. It's because he did it. He did it for Lindsay when he was home over Christmas break. He went through my emails and compared all of my friends' addresses with the Boyfriend Whisperer's IP address, and yours hit. I called him last night and asked him about it, and he admitted it."

"But why?"

"Ah." She waves her hand in the air. "He's always had a thing for Lindsay. No doubt she sweet-talked him into it. She knew he'd be able to figure something out, and the fact that he had access to all of my accounts made it that much easier."

"No, I mean, why would she go to that much trouble to figure out who I was?"

Abi looks at me as though I'm a dimwit. "Because Ty and Alicea? Hello?"

"Oh, wow." I sink onto the footstool. Suddenly it all makes sense. Lindsay must have liked Ty when I whispered him for Alicea, so she set out to figure out who the Boyfriend Whisperer was. At some point, she figured out I had a crush on Chris, so she decided to revenge date him. Not only that, she hired me to whisper him for her. "Lindsay Freaking LaDouche," I mutter. A knot forms in my stomach as I realize that Lindsay truly did use Chris to get back at me. She led him on, played with him, cheated on him, humiliated him. And all of it is my fault.

"Lexi, I'm so sorry," Abi says. "I know I complained a lot about this job, but I never meant for anything like this to happen."

"No, you're not to blame. I am." I hug my knees into my chest. I caused all those broken hearts out there on the other side of the closet, including Chris's. "You were right all along. I was messing with people's emotions. Me. The last person in the world who should be giving advice about love. I'm such an idiot."

"Don't say that." Abi wraps her arms around me. "And don't worry. Chris will forgive you."

I offer her half of my Power Bar, and we sit in silence for a while, each lost in our own thoughts. Mine are like a merry-go-round, minus the merry part. *Is Abi right? Will Chris forgive me? No way. I don't even think I can forgive myself. But maybe he will. Or not. Probably not. But maybe.*

"You have chem lab this afternoon, right?" Abi interrupts the madness.

"Yes. Don't remind me. I may skip and go to the nurse's office."

"No, you should go." Abi stands and paces back and forth in front of me. "Tell Chris you want to talk to him after school."

"What if he says no?"

"Insist."

"And what then?"

She stops and stares at me, her jaw set. "You tell him the truth. About everything."

"Everything?"

"Everything."

"Including the fact that I like him?"

"Everything."

Chapter
FIFTY-FIVE

Chem lab is a repeat of a couple of weeks ago, only worse. Things were awkward then, but now they're downright hostile. The air is as tense as a tightrope ready to snap. Chris and Lindsay. Chris and me. The entire class and me.

Chris actively ignores me as he sets up the materials for our experiment, which has something to do with magnets. How am I supposed to ask him to meet me after school if I can't even get him to look at me?

While Ms. Gupta drones on about attraction and repulsion, I surreptitiously text Abi for support.

```
Lexi: i can't do it.
Abi: u can. u must.
Lexi: we're like two negatively charged
ions
```

```
Abi: ???
Lexi: repulsion
Abi: well, then, it's time to get
positive.
Lexi: >:(
Abi: lol turn that frown upside down
Abi: +++++
```

I look up to find Ms. Gupta hovering over me, still talking about ions, her hand extended. I surrender my phone without protest. The stupid thing is filled with hate messages anyway.

"Thank you, Miss Malloy. You can retrieve this after the last bell." Ms. Gupta slips the phone into her desk drawer and carries on while I bury my head in my arms on the lab table. I'm not in a participatory mood, and Chris seems more than happy to fly solo on this one.

I close my eyes and try to decide what to say to him. *We need to talk.* No. Too cliché. *Give me a chance to apologize.* Ugh. I couldn't handle it if he said no. *Might we have a word after school?* Way too formal. And … British sounding.

Crap. What is wrong with me? Chris has been my best friend since the third grade. I should be able to— Was that the bell? Double crap! I lift my head to find Chris halfway out the door. Part of me wants to let him go, but I know Abi's right. I have to do this.

"Chris, wait! Chris!" I take off after him. He either doesn't hear me or is ignoring me, but I catch up with him in the hallway and step in front of him, blocking his way. "Hey."

"Hey." He steps backward. He is literally repelled by me.

"I ... can we ... give me a chance to explain."

"I gotta get to class." He tries to step around me, but I won't let him. He sighs. "Let me by."

"I'll come over to your house after school. It won't take long. Hear me out, and then you can ignore me all you want." I take a deep breath. People are staring, but I don't care. I lean forward and plead. "We've been friends forever. You can't throw that away without letting me tell you my side of things. Please."

He fakes to the left and passes me on the right. Man. How did I fall for that? "Please?" I shout after him.

"Fine," he calls over his shoulder. "After school."

Chris's mom smiles when she opens the door. "Lexi! What a nice surprise. It's been a while, hasn't it?" She gives me a long hug. "Chris is downstairs. I'm sure he'll be happy to see you."

Right. I thank her, take a deep breath, and head toward the basement. Chris is sitting on the couch with his eyes closed, ear buds in, so he doesn't notice me at first.

I stand nervously for a moment, taking him in. He's the same boy I've known for eight long years, yet so different.

A series of images flash through my mind—times we've wrestled on that couch, made forts out of its cushions, sat on it to play crazy eights or go fish or war. Once when we were about eleven years old, I did a backflip over the side, and my shirt flew up. I'd just started wearing a bra, and though Chris pretended he didn't see it, I knew he did. I wanted to die. After that, we stuck to playing board games and watching movies. There was no more rough-housing, no physical contact at all except the occasional bump and run on the court, and even then, I could tell he was holding back.

He opens his eyes and jumps. "Jeez, Lexi! How long have you been standing there?"

I shrug and sit down carefully next to him as he pulls out his earbuds. "I just got here. What are you listening to?"

"Dark Side of the Moon. Kind of matches my mood."

"I'm sorry. About ... everything."

Chris stares into the distance and says nothing.

I clasp my hands together and clear my throat. "I'm going to start at the beginning." Chris sets his jaw but says nothing, so I press on. "Remember that day way back in September when Abi pulled me out of the cafeteria?"

I tell him everything. Well, almost everything. I tell him about Abi and Briggsy, and the founding of Boyfriend Whisperer Enterprises, and how I was thinking about franchising it and how I'm not sure I want to play college hoops. I explain about Ty and Alicea, and Jolene and Brendon, and all the other couples. I tell him about Lindsay's application, and the pheromone experiment, and the Teddy bear with the Bulls jersey, and how I found Lindsay and Ty together, and how I'm really, really sorry for keeping so much from him for so long and how I don't blame him if he hates me. But I don't tell him how I feel. I can't. Because as I'm talking, Chris's expression goes from apathetic to annoyed to angry and back to apathetic. It's the apathy I can't face.

Finally, he turns toward me and speaks, his eyes guarded, his voice calm. "I need to know one thing."

"Okay."

"When you set me up with Lindsay, was that ... was it purely because it was your job, or did you want us to be together, or what?"

"I thought she liked you. And I could tell you liked her. I wanted you to be happy." I'm dying to reach out and grab his hands, but instead, I tug at a loose thread on one of the couch pillows, twisting it around and around my pinkie. "If I'd known Lindsay was going to do what she did Saturday night, I never would have accepted her application. You have to believe that."

Chris nods, but his expression is sad. Disappointed. "I believe you."

I can't bear to have him look at me like this. "I was trying to be a good friend, Chris. I swear. That's all I wanted." *It about killed me, but it's true.*

Chris offers a small smile. "Okay. I get it." He's being nice, but something has changed. He's pulling back. Shutting down.

"Well, thank you for listening. And for not totally hating me?"

"Of course not. I never *totally* hated you." He gives me a sideways smile, and though I know he's teasing, it still hurts. Guess I deserve that.

We sit in silence for a moment and then, with a burst of incredulity, Chris throws his hands in the air. "In other news … did you just say you don't want to play college ball? What's that about? And what will your parents say?"

I groan and lean back into the couch. "Don't remind me. Mom just bought us tickets to go up to U Conn."

"U Conn? You got an offer from U Conn?" Chris sits up and faces me, his mouth agape. "Lexi, that's huge."

I wave away his enthusiasm. "It's not a full. And Dad says there's no way I'd start freshman year and probably not even sophomore year. And I'm not even sure I want to play, remember? So, not so huge."

"How can you not want to play? I don't get it."

"I didn't say I don't want to play; I said I'm not sure." I hug the pillow to my chest. How do I explain this to someone whose entire goal in life is to play ball? I speak slowly, haltingly, partly because I'm trying to figure it out myself. "It's like … just because I can play, does it mean I have to? Mom keeps saying I have a gift, but does that make it my destiny? Does it mean I have to spend the next five years—not just during the season, but every single break and all my summers—practicing and training and stressing about basketball? What if I want to study abroad for a year, or do an internship somewhere, or … take up macramé? College is supposed to be a time to figure things out."

Chris shakes his head. "Wow. I had no idea."

I bite my lip and take a chance. "And what if I didn't

want to go to college at all?"

His eyes widen. "Are you serious?"

"Maybe. I don't know. I thought I wanted to franchise Boyfriend Whisperer Enterprises right after high school, but that's obviously not happening. But what if there's something else? I want options. And right now, with all these schools trying to get me to commit, I feel like I'd be giving up my options." I sigh. "Sorry. I'm sure I sound like an ungrateful loser."

"No." Chris shakes his head. "I mean, sure, I'd give my right arm to have your problems, but it's wild to hear you say all this. I never knew. I always figured you were Lexi Malloy, the Girl Who Has It All Figured Out."

Tears spring to my eyes, and I look away. I've always let everyone believe that. I've wanted to believe it myself. Chris is the first person I've ever confessed all this to, and part of me would love to tell him the rest of the story as well, to spill everything and tell him about the thing I want most in the world. But I don't. I can't.

Chapter
FIFTY-SIX

"You didn't tell him?" Abi places her hand on her hip and shakes her head.

"Watch out!"

We both jump to miss the foam ball someone has thrown our way. We're playing dodgeball in gym, and Abi and I seem to be everyone's favorite targets. Still, it's nice to be able to talk to her out in the open without having to stress about what people think.

"I couldn't. Honestly, I'm just glad he's still talking to me. I think we might even get back to being friends. Nothing would make me happier."

"Mmm hmm." Abi pops an exaggerated head weave. "Don't even try that on me, girlfriend." She ducks to avoid another ball.

"Hey! No head shots!" I stomp over to the dude who

threw it. "What do you think you're doing? Apologize."

Abi waves him off. "Forget it, Lexi. Not worth it."

"No. I mean it." I turn toward the crowd watching us. "You can throw the stupid ball at me all you want, but leave Abi out of it. She never did anything to you. She was my assistant, and she's ..." I glance at her. "My friend, but I was the one who called the shots. I'm the one who supposedly ruined your lives."

"Supposedly?" Annie Blevins, a short red-headed girl with big eyes and a mouth to match, steps forward. I set her up New Year's Eve with a guy from her English class. "You still don't get it, do you? You took our money and screwed us over. Did you really think coaching me to become a huge football fan overnight was going to work? Did you honestly believe knowing the stats of the entire Redskins offensive line was going to be my ticket to true love?"

I draw myself up to my full five feet, nine inches and glare down at Annie. "Yes, actually, I did. And so did you." I wave my finger at the whole group. "So did all of you. And you were happy to go along with it as long as it worked. So maybe it didn't last. And maybe I screwed up. Fine. Hate me if you want, but I was trying to help. I was trying to help you find love, and if that's a crime, well, I guess I'm guilty as charged." I turn and stalk away toward the girls' locker room. I've dodged enough balls for one day.

I change in the very back of the room, hoping to avoid everyone, but it's no use. As I'm fastening the belt to my jeans, Alicea Springer corners me.

"Lexi?"

I sigh and sink down onto the nearest bench. Here we

go. "Alicea, I'm not in the mood. I know you're pissed, and you have every right to be, and I'm sorry. I really am. I'm sorry I did such a crappy job setting you up, I'm sorry you and Ty broke up right before prom, and I'm really, truly sorry for the way things turned out with him and Lindsay."

"Well, I appreciate that, but—"

"But what?" I tear up, and my voice cracks. Damn it. The last thing I want is to let my classmates see me cry, but a girl can only take so much. "You're just dying to tell me how much I screwed up your life, aren't you? You want to pile on? Fine. Bring it. Bring the hate."

"Actually, that's not why I'm here." Alicea sits down next to me. "I'm here to thank you."

Thank me?

"I was always super shy around guys. I never knew what to say, or how to say it. I worried so much about sounding stupid; I wouldn't say anything at all. In fact, I did the same thing around girls, adults, little kids, pretty much everyone. But you changed all that."

"Me?"

"Yes. You and your emails." She gazes off into the distance and recites, "*You're beautiful and brilliant, and you have a voice that matters. Now use it!* Sound familiar?"

I nod. I don't remember typing those exact words, but it sounds like something the Boyfriend Whisperer would have said, especially to someone as quiet and withdrawn as Alicea.

"I read those words over and over until I believed them. And they worked. They got me to talk to Ty. Not only that, I made friends with a few girls in my dance class, and I even aced my oral report in poli-sci last week. Mr. Bartlett said I spoke with passion and conviction. Me!"

"Wow, that's awesome. That's amazing." I remember Chris's crack that night at Italiano's about Alicea having more face time with her computer than with guys. Did my emails really give her that kind of confidence?

Alicea grabs my hands in hers. "I mean it. Thank you. You've changed my life."

I smile and give her a long, tight hug. Maybe Boyfriend Whisperer Enterprises did some good after all.

Chapter
FIFTY-SEVEN

Mom opens her laptop and pulls up her spreadsheet on colleges. "I'm rating U Conn's offer a five out of ten, but I'm giving that assistant coach a nine. She was a sharp lady. Very impressive. Now, let's see … the campus. How would you rate that?"

I play with the food tray fastener on the seatback in front of me. "It was nice."

"Nice. Is that a seven? An eight? I need a number."

Mom, Dad, and I are sitting on the tarmac waiting to go home from our weekend visit to U Conn. Mom has the window seat, Dad is on the aisle answering emails, and I'm stuck in the middle trying to work up the nerve to spill what I've wanted to tell them for months. Maybe I'll wait until we take off. Mom wouldn't dare create a scene thirty thousand feet in the air on a packed flight, would she? People get arrested for that kind of thing. On the other hand, maybe that's not such a great plan.

"Mark, what do you think?"

"I think I'm going to fire Paul when I get back to the office. He let a major deal slip through our fingers. I can't go away for two days without everything falling apart."

"Oh, put away your phone." Mom swats at him across my lap. "I want to record this while it's fresh in our minds. What did you think of the campus?"

I reach over and shut her laptop. "I have something I need to tell you."

Mom's eyes widen as she looks from me to her computer and back again. "What on earth?"

"It's about college, and basketball, and … options."

"Yes, options." Mom points to her laptop. "That's precisely why I put together this spreadsheet. So we can assess your options and figure out which one is best."

I nod slowly. "We're on the same page … kind of. Except, I'm not sure any of those are best."

"What do you mean?" Mom clasps the armrest between us. "Is there another offer you haven't told us about? Is it Syracuse? Oh, Mark, wouldn't that be something? Your alma mater."

"No, no. It's not Syracuse. It's not another offer."

"Then what?"

I take a deep breath and answer slowly, carefully. "What if we expanded our vision a bit? Looked at all the possible options. Including … not playing basketball."

"What?" Dad's shout draws stares from the couple across the aisle.

"Oh, good lord. Are you pregnant?"

"What? No. Mom. What?"

"Bev."

"Why else would she quit basketball?"

"It's a phase. Trust me. I went through it myself in high school. Thought maybe I'd like to take a year off before college. She'll get over it."

I wave my hand between their faces. "Hello? I'm right here."

"She'd better, and soon. These schools aren't going to wait forever on her decision."

"I'm right here! And it's not a phase. It's a serious proposition. I'm not saying I won't play ball. I'm saying I want to at least consider what my future might look like if I didn't."

"Well." My mom huffs and shakes her head. "I don't understand it. Has that Gerald boy been putting ideas in your head?"

"It's Jerod. And he has nothing to do with this."

"Then where is it coming from? Not play basketball? You love basketball."

I rest my head against my seat back. "I do. It's just … I don't know if I want the next five years of my life to revolve around it. Maybe there are bigger and better things out there for me."

Even as I say it, doubt creeps in. What things? Certainly not Boyfriend Whisperer Enterprises.

"Honey, do yourself a favor. Sign with one of these schools." My dad rubs his knee. "A lot of high school athletes go through this, but it'll pass, and you'll be glad you did the smart thing."

I clench my teeth. He's a cliché. Maybe I'm a cliché, too. The Spoiled High School Star Who Can't Commit. "Can't we at least entertain the idea that I might have other aspirations in life?"

"Such as?" Mom asks. "What are these future plans? They must be quite grand since they apparently leave no room for the one thing you've spent your whole life training for."

"That's just it!" I point at her. Finally, someone has put into words what's been bothering me.

"What's it?"

"I've been training all my life for one thing. And I appreciate it. I do. I know both of you have sacrificed a lot so I could play. But maybe I want to try some other things. Who knows? Maybe I'd be good at acting or vlogging or, say … running a business. How will I know if I have to spend all my time on the court?

"You're exaggerating." Mom purses her lips. "You heard Coach Morris. You'll have your classes and your homework and …" Her voice trails off.

"Right. And that's about it. There's no time for anything else."

"You know, when I was in college, I spent all my spare time waitressing so I could afford to be there. You wouldn't have to work at all. Yet you want to turn your nose up at a scholarship?"

I close my eyes. Part of me wants to give in and say they're right and tell them I'd rate the stupid campus a seven. It would be so much easier. But I can't. I can't let them control my fate. "I know this isn't what you want to hear, but it's my life, my future. If it includes basketball, it will be because I've decided I want to play, not because other people expect me to."

Mom blinks hard. "Young lady, you'd better—"

The flight attendant appears in the aisle directly in front of our row and starts demonstrating how to fasten our seat belts and put on our oxygen masks. We sit in silence as she pantomimes to a recording of the instructions, but I can feel my mother steaming beside me.

Finally, as she finishes, Dad clears his throat. "You need to give this some serious thought, Lexi. You've worked hard to get to this point. Don't throw it away for no good reason."

I grab his hand. "I will. I promise." I turn to my mom. "I'm not doing this to hurt you, Mom. I swear. I'm just trying to figure stuff out. Whatever I decide, I hope you'll support me. But regardless, I'm going to make this decision myself, and I'm going to do what makes sense for me."

Chapter
FIFTY-EIGHT

"You said that? To your mom?" Chris gapes at me from across the booth at Italiano's. He has a dab of tomato sauce on the side of his lips and I'm dying to reach over and wipe it off, but I force myself to stay focused.

"It made for a tense flight home, but she'll get over it."

Chris shakes his head. "I don't know. We're talking about your mom. The same woman who took away your phone for three weeks freshman year for talking back to her."

"Meh." I nibble at my crust. "She's already coming around."

"Really?"

"Yep. As I left to come here tonight, she yelled at me to drive carefully. It's the first thing she's said since we got back. I take it as progress."

"What about your dad?"

I shrug. "He's a little easier. He'll be okay."

Chris gives me a sly grin. "How many times did he rub his bad knee on that flight?"

I laugh and roll my eyes. "I counted sixteen. Which is about fourteen times more than on the flight up."

Chris finally wipes his mouth with his napkin, and I take a deep breath. I asked him to come out tonight for a reason, and it wasn't to talk about my trip to U Conn. Standing up to my parents was tough, but it has made all the difference. I feel like I can breathe, and I've been dream-free for two nights. I've decided I need to clear the air one more time. I may not be able to tell Chris everything, but I do want to have a heart-to-heart with him about one thing.

"Remember the last time we were here?"

Chris squints as though he's trying to place it.

"I was sitting in my car, and you knocked on my window?"

"Oh, yeah. I still don't understand why you were ordering on your—" He stops, and his eyes light up. "Wait a minute. You were on a stakeout, weren't you? Spying on someone. Who was it?" He cranes his neck and checks out the front window as though Brendon McDonough might still be sitting there four months later, slopping down his pizza.

"Not important." I give a dismissive wave of my hand. I won't discuss clients or cases. Just because I was outed doesn't mean their dirty laundry needs to be. "What's important is something you said to me that night. I don't know if you'll remember it, but …" I blink hard and tug at my straw. "It pissed me off."

Chris leans across the table, his expression serious. "What did I say?" The concern in his voice is so palpable that part of me already regrets bringing it up. It was an offhand comment. Why make a big deal about it? Only it was more than that.

"It was about me being a girl ... or not. And—"

"Oh, right. I remember." Chris taps his forehead. "I'm sorry. I know what I said, and it was stupid. I mean, you *were* acting a little weird, but I get it now. Super spy and all." He must read the confusion on my face because he holds up his hands to stop me from replying and rushes on. "But even if you didn't have a reason to act weird, I shouldn't have said it. It was sexist. And even if it *wasn't* sexist, I probably shouldn't have said it, because you're allowed to have weird moments. Or days. Or weeks. I had no right to judge. I suck."

I squint, trying to process his apology. "Okay. But ... what exactly are you talking about?"

"That night. When I asked if you were ... whether you were having your ...?"

"Ohhhh." Of course. His remark about me acting like it was that time of the month. I'd forgotten all about it. I close my eyes and press the heels of my palms into my eyes. How did he go from asking me about my period one minute to insinuating I'm not even a girl the next? "That's not what I was talking about. I mean, I appreciate the apology, though, 'cause that was kind of a rude thing to ask."

He pulls my hands from my face. "What then? What did I say?"

I swallow hard, look him straight in the eyes, and spit it out. "You said you didn't think I was a girl."

"No way."

"You said it. Right there in that booth." I point to where we were sitting that night.

He furrows his brow in thought and shakes his head. "No. I remember what I said, and that wasn't it. Or at least, that wasn't what I meant. Believe me, Lexi, I am well aware of your sex. I mean, your gender. Your ... your ...." He waves in the general direction of my body. "Girl-ness."

I feel my face grow warm, but I press on. "So then what did you say? Or mean? Because it sure felt like you meant you didn't think of me as a girl."

Chris pushes aside his plate and his drink and rests his forearms on the table between us. "I believe my exact words were something along the lines of, 'It's almost like *you* think you're a girl.' Because sometimes it seems like you ... I don't know. Fight it."

"Being a girl?"

"Yeah."

"That's ridiculous."

"Is it?"

"Yes. Just because I don't own a single piece of pink clothing, and I can't apply eyeliner without looking like a raccoon, and I'd rather be on the court than at the mall, and I basically don't do any of the stuff girls are supposedly always doing, doesn't mean I'm fighting it. I'm ... redefining it."

He grins. "Fair enough." His eyes grow soft, and I realize he's staring at me the same way he did that day on Massey's staircase. "Whatever you're doing, it's working."

Redefined or not, the girl in me melts under his gaze. My face, my neck, my whole body burns. I open my mouth, but nothing comes out.

Chris motions toward the door. "Want to get out of here?"

Chapter
FIFTY-NINE

Claymore Park is empty. And dark. Two of the streetlights are out, and if it weren't for a full moon, we wouldn't be able to see the basket.

Chris shows off his newest skill, dribbling behind his back, while I stand between him and the net. I rest my hands on my hips and cock my head. He's got to make a move sometime. He approaches me slowly, smiling, still dribbling.

He fakes to the right, but I don't fall for it, and in the blink of an eye, I have the ball. I take it out and rush back, but halfway through my layup, I realize he's stopped chasing me. I glance over to see what's wrong, and the ball bounces off the rim. "What's the matter?"

He shrugs. "Nothing. Just admiring redefined femininity in action."

I'm glad it's dark, so he can't see me blush. I look around for the ball, but it has rolled off somewhere into the grass.

He strolls over to me. It's a cool night, but we've been playing hard, and I can feel the heat radiating off his body. "I get it, you know." His eyes search mine. "Not wanting to sign with a college team. It's like me deciding to do the Polar Plunge."

I frown. "You mean you think I'm suffering from temporary insanity?"

Chris laughs. "No. Don't you see? The Plunge was never really about plunging. It was about seizing the moment. Breaking out."

"Breaking out?"

"Yeah. Out of the box everybody puts me in. The lame-o-dude-who's-always-in-Lexi-Malloy's-shadow box. I wanted to do something … different. Mine."

I nod. His face glistens in the moonlight, and his cowlick is sticking up in a most non-lame-o way. I have an urge to reach up and run my fingers through it, but I resist. "Is that what 'Happy Birthday' and the whole breakdance-ninja thing was about, too?"

He shrugs. "Maybe."

"For the record, I've never thought you were lame. And you're too tall to fit in my shadow."

He smiles. "For the record, I don't think of you as just an amazing basketball player. I think of you as … Lexi."

The way he says it makes my heart pound inside my chest. I feel like he means *me*—who I really am, who I've always been, and who I have the potential to be. I swear no one has ever said my name like that before, and it makes me want to put my arms around his neck and kiss him. I want to tell him I'm so, so thankful he's my best friend and that I'm lucky to have him in my life and am totally and completely in love with him. But I don't. Instead, I laugh and give an exaggerated twirl as if to show off the fabulosity that is Lexi.

Chris grins and takes a step closer to me. For a moment, I imagine he's going to kiss me, but then he looks away. "Now, where did that ball go?" He shuffles off into the darkness to find it.

Crap. I should have said it. If I were one of my clients, I'd tell myself to woman up and do it. I'd tell myself I was being a total freaking wimp and I was never going to find love if I couldn't get it together. What is it they say? Those who can't do, teach. That's me. *Come on, Lexi. Stop being such a … lame-o.*

Wait a minute. Who am I kidding? That's not what I'd say to a client at all. I'd never call one of them a wimp or lame. No, if I were one of my clients, I'd remind myself that I'm strong and smart and beautiful and have arms other girls would kill for. I'd tell myself I'm a rock star. Lexi. The way Chris said it.

"Heads up." Chris appears at the edge of the court and tosses the ball to me. It's damp from the grass.

I dribble slowly, purposefully toward him. *Go for it, Lexi. You can't score unless you take the shot.* "Remember the last time we were here, and you asked me about the dodgeball thing?"

Chris looks down at his feet. "Yeah?"

"It wasn't a pity pick."

"Okay."

I stop dribbling and tuck the ball under my arm. "I did it because I wanted you on my team. Because we *are* a team."

Chris's eyes meet mine. His expression is curious, as

though he's wondering where I'm going with this.

"Don't get me wrong," I tease. "It might not have been the smartest move at the time. But it was real. I chose you. I still choose you. I want you to know that."

He squints. "What are you saying, Lexi?"

I squeeze my eyes shut and exhale. "I'm saying win or lose, I'm lucky to have you. And I'm saying ...." I twirl the ball between my two pointer fingers as my mom's voice echoes inside my head. *You might not be here if your father hadn't made the first move. I couldn't do it. Wouldn't do it. I was too chicken.* I can't let fear keep me from doing something this important, something that could change everything. "I'm saying you're my best friend. And I want you to be my best friend forever. And maybe ... more."

For a long moment, Chris says nothing. My heart pounds inside my chest as I wait for him to respond. Was that a brave move? Or a stupid one? Finally, he takes a step toward me. "Want to know something?" His voice is low.

"What?"

He grabs the ball from me and tosses it back into the night. "The secret admirer? I kind of thought it was you. I kind of ... hoped it was you."

"Really?" My head swims and my legs feel weak, and I have to blink hard to clear my mind. "You did?"

"Yeah. I mean, right up until you basically shoved Lindsay at me."

So that bouquet was meant for me? My breath grows shallow as my mind processes how different the past few months might have been if I'd made a move on Chris myself rather than letting someone else hire me to do it for her.

How a teddy bear in a Bulls jersey from the right girl could have changed everything. How I sat on the bench and let someone else play my position and even cheered her on.

Chris takes my hands in his. How can he be so calm and steady when I'm shaking like a pompom at a pep rally? "You're my best friend, too, and I don't want to mess anything up between us, but—"

"Why did you sleep with her?" My hand flies to my mouth. Where did that come from? It's a question I hadn't planned to ask, and I'm not sure I want the answer.

"What?"

I pull my other hand away and look down. "Never mind. It's none of my business. You don't owe me an explanation. It's just … you said she was a great girl. That's the most you ever said. You never said you loved her or saw any kind of a future with her, but you slept with her and I didn't think you'd—"

"I didn't. We didn't."

"What?"

"I don't know what you're talking about. I liked Lindsay a lot, or at least, I liked the person I thought she was. I liked the idea of her, and I have to admit, I liked all the attention she gave me. But that was it. And we never …."

I take a deep breath and fight the tears that have sprung up out of nowhere. Of course. Revenge. Lindsay told me they'd slept together, or led me to believe it, to make me miserable. And it worked. I'm such an idiot. I shake my head. "I'm sorry. It was something Lindsay said. I shouldn't have listened."

I feel as though a huge weight has been lifted off me, a weight I didn't even realize had been crushing me. I reach out my hand, and Chris accepts it and pulls me back toward him. I rest the other hand on his stomach. It's a simple gesture, but it feels big, bold. "I don't want to mess us up, either, but I have a feeling it's too late for that." I sigh. "I have been incredibly stupid."

He strokes my cheek with the back of his hand. "Not stupid. Maybe … careful. And so have I. I'm tired of being careful."

"Yeah. Me too." I smile and do the most carefree thing I can think of and perhaps the most carefree thing I've ever done in my entire life. I stand on my tiptoes and kiss him—a sweet, soft kiss that sends my pulse racing. The sounds of traffic on Sterling Boulevard fade away as I taste his lips, warm and salty. The kiss is somehow simultaneously everything I've dreamed it would be yet nothing like I'd imagined. I'm grateful for his arms circling my waist, keeping me from dissolving into a puddle on the asphalt.

"That was … not messed up," he says.

"Not even a little bit." I step back and take in his silhouette against the moon. His broad shoulders and clean-shaven, chiseled chin. "Hey, can I …?" I reach up and run my fingers through his cowlick.

"What are you doing?" He laughs and swats my hand away.

"I've wanted to do that for so long. You have no idea."

"You have?"

"Yes."

"My cowlick?"

"It's sexy. Trust me."

He gives me a teasing grin. "Want to do it again?"

"Can I?"

He leads me to the bench at the side of the court and pulls me down next to him. Our legs are entwined, and he rests his hand on my knee as I play with his hair. Is this for real? I've wanted it for so long, imagined it, dreamed it, but I never quite believed it could happen.

"So you really thought I didn't see you as a girl?"

I nod.

"Lexi, I have always thought of you as a girl—as the prettiest, strongest, most incredible girl I know."

"You lie."

"It's true." He gazes into my eyes, and even without a fireplace nearby or his practice jacket around my shoulders, I feel warm all over. He takes my hands in his. "I didn't realize how much I wanted to be more than friends until the secret admirer thing, but I promise you, your girl-hood has never been in question."

I can't believe he's saying these things, and part of me wants to sit here and listen to him say them all night, but a bigger part wants nothing more than to feel his lips pressed against mine again, to repeat that incredible, beautiful kiss.

Love is but a whisper away.

"Kiss me," I whisper.

And so he does.

He kisses me once. He kisses me again. He kisses me a third time, and a fourth.

And then I lose count.

THE END

ACKNOWLEDGEMENTS

This book would not be possible without the hard work, support, and inspiration of so many. I am thankful to you all, and especially:

To Georgia McBride, the entire Swoon Romance team, and my agent, Andrea Somberg, who continue to believe in me.

To my many amazing writing friends, and especially to Ellen Braaf, Kathy Chappell, the Cudas, Tom Angleberger, Autumn Lala, the Writer's Center-Leesburg Committee members, the SCBWI Mid-Atlantic Chapter, the Romance Writers of America Virginia Chapter, and the Romance Writers of America Young Adult Chapter. You make the path wider, clearer, and a lot more fun.

To the Sports Junkies, with a special shout out to AWadd, for inspiring my idea for *The Boyfriend Whisperer* 2.0. (Yes, there will be a sequel.)

To the tweens and teens in the Sterling United Methodist Church LifeSigns youth group, and to the SUMC book clubs. Thanks for all the love.

To my parents, Bea and Ted Acorn, and my siblings, Deb Acorn, Karen Benfield, and Ted Acorn, for all their love and support.

To Joe and Eris and Sarah. I couldn't ask for a better family.

And to God, in whom all things are possible.

LINDA ACORN BUDZINSKI

Linda Budzinski is author of three young adult novels, *The Boyfriend Whisperer, Em & Em,* and *The Funeral Singer.* She lives in Northern Virginia with her husband, Joe, and their feisty Chihuahua, Demitria. She's a sucker for romance and reality TV and, of course, matchmaking, so she's been known to turn off her phone's ringer when watching *The Bachelor.* Her favorite flower is the daisy, her favorite food is chocolate, and her favorite song is "Amazing Grace." When she's not writing, she works in nonprofit communications and outreach.

OTHER SWOON ROMANCE TITLES YOU MIGHT LIKE

THE FUNERAL SINGER
EM & EM
THE BREAK UP SUPPORT GROUP
ONE SUMMER WITH AUTUMN

Find more awesome teen books like this at
http://www.myswoonromance.com/

Connect with Swoon Romance online:
Facebook: www.Facebook.com/swoonromance
Twitter: https://twitter.com/SwoonRomance
You Tube: https://www.youtube.com/swoonromance
Instagram: https://instagram.com/swoonromance/

THE *Funeral Singer*

LINDA BUDZINSKI

LINDA BUDZINSKI

She'll run away from her past and into his arms.
So what if it's all one big lie.

Em & Em

the
break♥up
support
group

a novel

cheyanne young

One Summer with Autumn

with

Autumn

Julie Reece